"The only reason I told you all this is that I want somebody else to know in case something happens to me."

"Why would something happen to you?"

"If he catches wind that I'm hunting him, then there's no question he'll come after me."

"I still want to be a part of this." Her chin shot up a notch and her eyes held a definite challenge.

"Don't make me regret I told you everything," Jake said. Damn, he should have never told her the names of the two men he suspected. That had been careless of him.

She reached out and covered his hand with hers, the unexpected pleasant touch sparking an electric jolt in him. "Please, Jake. Don't try to shut me out."

DESPERATE MEASURES

New York Times Bestselling Author

CARLA CASSIDY

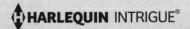

If you purchased this book without a cover you should be aware that this book is stolen property. It was reported as "unsold and destroyed" to the publisher, and neither the author nor the publisher has received any payment for this "stripped book."

PLEASE RECYCLE
THIS PRODUCT IS RECYCLABLE
Recycling programs for this product may not exist in your area.

ISBN-13: 978-1-335-60440-8

Desperate Measures

Copyright © 2019 by Carla Bracale

All rights reserved. Except for use in any review, the reproduction or utilization of this work in whole or in part in any form by any electronic, mechanical or other means, now known or hereafter invented, including xerography, photocopying and recording, or in any information storage or retrieval system, is forbidden without the written permission of the publisher, Harlequin Enterprises Limited, 22 Adelaide St. West, 40th Floor, Toronto, Ontario M5H 4E3, Canada.

This is a work of fiction. Names, characters, places and incidents are either the product of the author's imagination or are used fictitiously, and any resemblance to actual persons, living or dead, business establishments, events or locales is entirely coincidental.

This edition published by arrangement with Harlequin Books S.A.

For questions and comments about the quality of this book, please contact us at CustomerService@Harlequin.com.

® and TM are trademarks of Harlequin Enterprises Limited or its corporate affiliates. Trademarks indicated with ® are registered in the United States Patent and Trademark Office, the Canadian Intellectual Property Office and in other countries.

HARLEQUIN®
www.Harlequin.com

Printed in U.S.A.

Carla Cassidy is an award-winning, *New York Times* bestselling author who has written more than 120 novels for Harlequin. In 1995, she won Best Silhouette Romance from *RT Book Reviews* for *Anything for Danny*. In 1998, she won a Career Achievement Award for Best Innovative Series from *RT Book Reviews*. Carla believes the only thing better than curling up with a good book to read is sitting down at the computer with a good story to write.

Visit the Author Profile page at Harlequin.com.

CAST OF CHARACTERS

Jake Lamont—He believes his guilt and rage over his sister's murder unleashed a monster on the community.

Monica Wright—A blog reporter who wants to break the Vigilante Killer case wide open.

Clay Rogers—One of six men who entered into a murder pact gone wrong.

Matt Harrison—Are Jake and Monica his loose ends that need to be taken care of?

Larry Albright—How angry is he with Monica and what might be his revenge?

Adam Kincaid—The creator of the murder pact. Is he the Vigilante Killer?

Chapter One

"And the winner of this year's most innovative design in the Kansas City area goes to Jake Lamont of Lamont and Star Architects Incorporated," the emcee for the night announced.

Jake rose as the people in the ballroom stood and clapped. He pasted on a fake smile, the same one he'd been wearing for the past couple of years, and made his way to the podium to retrieve the large shiny trophy.

He wove through the white-draped tables holding the remnants of a dinner that had consisted of a piece of dry chicken with a strange, mysterious green sauce over the top and potatoes and purple cauliflower on the side.

The meal had been horrible. The night already seemed endless, and he knew after the official itinerary was over there was still a cocktail party that would be filled with congratulations and glad-handing.

He should be thrilled with the recognition he'd

just received, but it was an empty victory without Suzanna standing by his side. Unfortunately, she couldn't stand beside him because she was dead. He shoved these painful thoughts away as he accepted his award with a short speech.

Twenty minutes later he stood in a circle of other architects talking about the huge renewal projects taking place in the Kansas City downtown district.

"I've got to admit it, your building at Tenth and Main is a real visual beauty," John Davis said. "And you're working on another one, aren't you?"

Jake nodded. "Third and Main is also mine."

"That's going to be some addition to the skyline," Richard Burke said. "What is it? Eighteen... twenty stories high?"

"Actually, it's twenty-two stories," Jake replied.

He stiffened slightly as Tim Lathrop joined the group. Jake and the dark-haired man with his cold blue eyes were often in competition for a job, and Tim had a reputation for not always playing nice.

"You know that award should have gone to me," he said.

"You can take it up with the members of the committee if you think a mistake was made," Jake replied.

Suddenly he was exhausted. He was tired of the fake smile he'd sported all night long. He wanted to rip off his gray-and-black tie and get out of his black suit and into something casual. The polite social chatter was wearing on him. He had so many other important things on his mind…things like murder.

It took another half an hour before he finally took his leave. He stepped out of the building where the celebration had been held and into the oppressively hot late-August night air. He made his way to his car parked down the block and as he walked he yanked to loosen the tie around his neck.

He couldn't wait to get home in his own space. All he wanted at the moment was a drink and his recliner, where he didn't have to smile or interact with anyone.

This was the first real social event he'd attended in the past two years and he'd found it beyond exhausting. He wouldn't have attended at all if it hadn't been for him receiving an award.

He'd only gone a short distance when a female voice called out from behind him. He turned and saw a petite, dark-haired woman hurrying toward him.

He frowned. She looked vaguely familiar, but he couldn't quite place her and in any case had no idea what she wanted with him. She wasn't one of the attendees of the night's festivities, for instead of wearing a cocktail dress she was clad in tight blue jeans and a royal blue tank top.

Despite her casual dress, she was quite attractive, but when she drew closer to where he stood beneath a streetlamp, recognition slammed into his gut.

Monica Wright. Oh, hell no. What was she doing here? The last person he wanted anywhere in his life was the investigative reporter with her popular podcast. And why did she want to speak to him?

"Mr. Lamont, could I just have a moment of your time?" She finally reached where he stood.

Despite his initial impulse to turn and hurry away, he smiled at her and played dumb. "And you are…?" He looked at her quizzically.

"Monica Wright of *The Wright News* podcast." She offered him a bright smile.

He'd found her attractive when he occasionally tuned in to her podcast, but in person she was even prettier. She was petite and shapely. Her eyes appeared more blue, a startling and beautiful contrast to her long dark hair. She had a heart-shaped face and full lips that were more than a little bit appealing.

"I see you brought home the big prize," she said with a gesture to the large trophy he held.

He relaxed. Maybe that's why she wanted to speak to him. "Yes, I'm very honored."

"The building you won for is a real beauty."

"Thank you. It's always nice when people recognize your hard work."

"And how did you feel when Max Clinton was murdered two nights ago?"

He stiffened, gut-punched by the unexpected question. "No comment." He turned on his heel and once again headed in the direction of his car.

"Mr. Lamont, I'd really like you to come on my podcast. I'm sure you have an interesting story to share."

She followed him like an annoying, yappy Chihuahua. "You must have some thoughts and feelings about Max Clinton being murdered by the Vigilante Killer."

Thankfully by that time he'd reached his car. He opened the door. He then turned back to face her. "I told you no comment and that's all I have to say on the matter." He got into the car and slammed the door.

He ignored her presence as he started his engine and then roared out of the parking lot. He headed north and tried to keep his mind empty.

But of course, that was impossible. With a single question, Monica Wright had stirred up a lot of thoughts…all of them bad. Why had she singled him out? Had she talked to some of the other men who had found their personal justice through a pact forged in hell? How had she possibly learned about them…about him? The last thing he wanted was to get tangled up in any discussion concerning the Vigilante Killer.

Home was a four-bedroom brick house on an acre of land. He'd had it built three years ago. At that time, he'd believed the bedrooms would eventually be filled with children. He didn't believe that anymore. He hadn't believed in anything like happiness or family since he'd lost his sister.

He pulled into his garage and then entered the kitchen, where he placed the trophy on the countertop. Eventually it would find its way into his downtown office, but not right now.

The first thing he did was head to his bedroom, where he changed out of the suit and into a pair of jogging pants and a T-shirt. He went into the family room and to the minibar in the back corner. He poured himself two fingers of Scotch over ice, and collapsed in his black leather recliner.

He took a sip of the drink, leaned his head back and closed his eyes. Instantly, a vision of Suzanna filled his head. Whenever he thought of her, it was with her head thrown back and her eyes twinkling with laughter.

She'd been so beautiful, with her short dark hair

and sparkling green eyes. She'd had an exuberance, a love of life that had been intoxicating to the people around her. She'd been the star in Lamont and Star. She'd been Jake's inspiration, his partner and his twin sister. And since her murder two years ago, Jake had been utterly lost.

He took another drink as his thoughts shifted to Max Clinton, the man who had killed Suzanna. He'd been Suzanna's boyfriend. He should have been her champion, the man who had her back, and instead he had beaten and strangled her in a fit of jealous rage. Unfortunately, his lawyer had managed to put enough doubt in the minds of the jury that he'd walked away a free man.

How did he feel when he'd learned that Max was the latest victim of the person the news had labeled the Vigilante Killer? He'd felt so many emotions that it had been difficult to sort them all out.

There had been the intense relief that Max Clinton would never again be in a position to hurt another woman. There had also been a renewed grief as Max's murder had caused a rush of memories to torment him…memories of his beautiful sister's life and torturous memories of the brutality of her death.

Two nights ago, Max had been killed by the Vigilante Killer, who liked slitting his victim's throats and then carving a deep V into their foreheads. Some would call Max's death karma, but Jake knew better.

Max's murder had come out of a meeting of Jake and five other grieving, angry men who had entered an agreement that assured them each a place in hell.

Finally, Max's murder had evoked a chilling, confirming fear as Jake recognized that he and those men had unleashed a monster on the community.

MONICA CURSED BENEATH her breath as she slit the tip of her finger on a piece of paper. So far, she was having a horrible morning and it was only nine o'clock.

She'd been up far too late the night before, waiting for her police department source to return her call. She wanted anything new he might have on the Vigilante Killer. Unfortunately, he hadn't returned her call.

Then first thing this morning her single-serve coffee machine had gasped and sputtered and refused to give up a cup of coffee. Her shower had spurted out only a trickle and had reminded her she'd been meaning to buy a new shower head. And when she walked outside to retrieve her morning paper, she stepped squarely in a pile of fresh dog poo.

And now this…a tiny cut that hurt like hell and refused to stop bleeding. She grabbed a tissue from the box on her desk and wrapped it around her finger, then leaned back in her chair and released a sigh of frustration.

And the source of her frustration wasn't the events of the morning, but rather that she hadn't been able to get Jake Lamont to be on her podcast that evening.

He would have made a compelling guest. He was the only surviving member of his family after his twin sister had been brutally murdered. The alleged perpetrator had walked scot-free and then two years later was murdered by a killer who seemed to be on a bloody journey of justice denied in the Kansas City area.

So far the police had admitted this particular killer had murdered four men, each of whom had been suspects in heinous crimes and each of whom had walked free due to glitches in the judicial process. And the killer seemed to be on a fairly fast track—four kills in less than two months and with no end in sight. So far he'd left no clues behind for the authorities to follow.

Monica wanted to be the one to break the case wide open. It was a lofty aspiration for a woman who had a nightly news podcast with just over twenty thousand subscribers and news that focused on the Kansas City and surrounding areas.

She wanted to break the case not only in hopes of expanding her visibility, but also to quiet the self-doubt that had driven her for most of her life. She needed to prove to her father that...

She jumped as her landline rang. She never answered this phone. It was a tips line of sorts that she advertised each evening when she ended her show.

So far, she'd received eleven marriage proposals, countless invitations to be a baby mama and several phone calls that had offered her the chance to be involved in strange sexual situations.

Lately she'd also been getting calls from Larry Albright, a local contractor. Monica had done an exposé on him three days ago when it came to light that he was scamming people out of thousands of dollars.

In the past two days he'd left dozens of nasty and threatening messages for her. She now chewed on the nail of the index finger that didn't have the paper cut on it as she waited to see who was calling this time.

"Hi, Monica. My name is Janet McCall. You don't know me, but I'm a huge fan of yours. Uh... but that's not why I'm calling. I know you've been asking for any information anyone might have concerning the Vigilante Killer."

The woman paused and Monica leaned forward, the paper cut on her finger forgotten. "This might be nothing at all and I could be wasting your time. I run the Northland Survivor Group and I just thought it was an odd coincidence that the Vigilante Killer has killed four men who perpetrated crimes against four of the men who attended my group for a short period of time."

Monica picked up the phone. "Janet, it's Monica Wright."

"Oh… I didn't expect to speak to you in person." She released a nervous laugh. "I'm a huge fan of yours."

"Thank you, I appreciate it, but I want to make sure I understand what you're telling me."

"Okay…hmm…according to the reports, the Vigilante Killer's first victim was Brian McDowell, who beat Matt Harrison's mother to death. The second victim was Steven Winthrop, who raped and killed Nick Simon's wife. The third kill was of Dwight Weatherby, who killed Troy Anderson's daughter, and now this fourth victim was Max Clinton, who beat and strangled Jake Lamont's sister. Matt Harrison, Troy Anderson, Nick Simon and Jake Lamont all belonged to the Northland Survivor Group for several months and then they all stopped coming to the meetings about the same time."

There was a long pause as Monica slowly digested the information. Janet gave another small, nervous laugh. "That was clear as mud, right?"

"Not at all, I'm just trying to wrap my mind around it," Monica replied. "Have you spoken to the police or any of the authorities about this?"

"No. I didn't really know if the information meant anything or not."

"Right now I don't know, either, but I'd like a little time to check into it before you give it to the police," Monica said.

"Of course," Janet replied slightly breathlessly. "So you think this might mean something?"

"To be honest, I don't know, but I really appreciate you bringing this to me."

Minutes later, Monica reared back in her chair, her mind racing with the information she'd just been given. Was it just a coincidence that the Vigilante Killer had murdered the bad guys of four men who attended a small survivors' group?

There were dozens of survivors' groups around the Kansas City area, yet according to what Janet had just told her, the Vigilante Killer had focused in on this particular group. Why?

And now she had another reason to talk to Jake Lamont. Although she couldn't see how this information worked in the puzzle she was trying to piece together, it definitely warranted further exploration. And that's what she did for a living.

For the rest of the morning she worked on the material for her podcast that night, and then she left the house to shop for a few groceries and to buy a new coffee machine. There was no way she was going to go a full day without her coffee.

It was nearly three by the time she got back home. The whole time she'd been shopping, her brain had worked overtime on the information Janet had given her. She made herself a cup of coffee and once again sat in her office chair.

Rather than thinking about the killer, she found herself thinking about Jake Lamont. He was definitely one hot hunk of a man. His suit had fit perfectly over his broad shoulders. His dark hair had been slightly shaggy and his eyes had been the deep green of a primal forest.

She'd come home the night before and had done a search on him. She'd learned that he was single and a successful architect. She'd reread articles about his sister's murder, and she'd also used a search engine that had provided both his work and home phone numbers and his home address.

At four she left her small ranch house and drove the fifteen miles to where Jake Lamont lived. She had no idea what time he got home from work. She didn't even know if he did work today, considering it was Saturday. But she intended to go to his house and try to talk to him again.

She especially wanted to speak to him now, armed with the new information she'd received from Janet. If he wasn't home when she arrived, then she intended to be there waiting for his return.

She still hoped to get him on her evening podcast and now she also wanted to ask him about the time he'd spent at the Northland Survivor Group and the other three men who had attended with him.

Jake's house was a large, beautiful brick with a huge bay window in the front. The lawn was neatly manicured, with trimmed bushes and flowers surrounding a beautiful fountain. Both the oversize plot and the expanse of the house whispered of money and success.

The first thing she did on arriving was knock on his front door. When there was no answer she assumed he wasn't home, and she pulled out of his circular driveway and parked down the street where she could see him when he arrived.

She'd taken him by surprise last night. She was hoping tonight he'd be more willing to talk with her. She'd just settled in to wait when her cell phone rang. There were only a few people who had this number.

Looking at the caller identification, her stomach instantly clenched tight with a familiar stress. "Hi, Dad," she answered.

"What are you doing?" Neil Wright's deep voice boomed over the line.

"I'm working."

Her father's dry chuckle twisted the nerves in her stomach even tighter. "I was hoping by the time you hit thirty you'd put that podcast silliness aside and get a real job."

"Dad, this is a real job," she replied, knowing it would do no good. She'd been a disappointment to her father since the moment she'd been born a girl instead of a boy.

She was the youngest of three girls and according to her father, was the last chance for him to get the son he'd desperately wanted.

It hadn't been so bad when her mother had been alive to soothe the hurt her father sometimes caused, but her mother had died from breast cancer when Monica had been eight.

"So, what's up?" she now asked.

"I'm heading out early in the morning for a day of fishing with Harry and Frank, but those parts I ordered for my truck came in at the Liberty location so I was wondering if while you're out running around tomorrow, you could pick them up for me."

Monica stifled a deep sigh. "Sure, I can do that."

"Great, just drop them off in the garage. I'll be home late tomorrow night."

When the call ended, she released the sigh she had stifled moments before. Her father often asked her to run errands for him and to her it was just another indication of how little he respected her and her job.

She knew she could gain his respect if she went back to school and became a nurse or a lawyer, like her two sisters had become.

But news was her passion and she absolutely loved what she did. Always in the back of her mind was the notion that if she became big enough, if she reached a certain number of followers or one of her stories got picked up by a national news source, maybe then she'd be good enough for her father to love.

All insecurities and thoughts of her father flew out of her head as Jake Lamont's car passed hers and turned into his driveway.

She started her engine and followed behind him, her heart beating with the excitement of a potential story. He stopped outside his garage door and got out of his car.

She quickly parked behind him and did the same. Good lord, the man had been a hunk in his suit last night, but he was even hotter in his jeans and a navy T-shirt that showcased his muscled chest and flat abdomen.

"You're trespassing." His handsome, chiseled features were taut with obvious anger.

"I thought with a night to think about it, maybe you changed your mind about being on my podcast." She offered him her most charming smile.

"My mind hasn't changed," he replied, and headed toward his front door.

She followed closely behind him. "Since the latest man murdered by the Vigilante Killer is tied to you and your sister's death, I'd really like to get how you feel about the murder on the record."

"What don't you understand about no comment?" he replied tersely. He unlocked his front door and then turned back to look at her. "And now it's time for you to get off my property."

"Just one more thing," she said hurriedly. "Can you confirm to me that you attended meetings at the Northland Survivor Group at the same time Nick Simon, Troy Anderson and Matt Harrison attended?"

He appeared to freeze. Once again he turned to face her. The anger that had ridden his features appeared to relax. "Okay, I'll give you five minutes. Come on in," he finally said, and to her surprise he opened his door wider.

Chapter Two

She'd shocked him. How in the hell had she managed to learn about the four men attending the Northland Survivor Group together? And what other information might she have?

His need to know what she knew was the only reason he invited her inside. Watching her podcast the few times he had, he'd recognized she was tenacious and ambitious...two dangerous traits when it came to her digging into the Vigilante Killer case.

He guessed the killer was one of two men, but he needed to know what Monica knew about the case, because if the truth came out he'd be charged as an accomplice.

Keep your friends close, but keep your enemies closer, he told himself as he ushered her into his family room. "Drink?" he asked as she eased down onto his sofa and he walked over to his minibar in the corner of the room. Maybe he could get her relaxed enough she would give up all the information she'd already gleaned about the case.

She gazed at him with a sudden wariness in the depths of her amazing blue eyes. "I just want you to know that my producer and my cameraman are in a car just up the street. Warren and Wally always have my back and they know I'm here. And with that said, I'd love a cold glass of water."

What did she think? That he'd invited her inside to kill her? He had no idea if she really had a Warren and Wally just waiting to run to her rescue, but he certainly had no intention of harming her in any way.

He handed her a glass of ice water and then carried his Scotch and water to the recliner chair opposite her. "Let's get one thing straight right now—I'm not going to be on your podcast," he began. "But I'll tell you off the record how I felt when I learned that Max Clinton was murdered by the Vigilante Killer."

"Do you mind if I record this?" She pulled a cell phone out of her oversize bright red purse.

"Actually, I do mind," he replied. He didn't want anything about this on tape. "I told you this was off the record. Besides, I'm not sure you need a recording for what I'm going to tell you. When I heard that Max Clinton had been murdered I felt nothing except for a bit of relief that he would never harm another woman again."

"Yes, I'm so sorry for your loss," she replied.

He nodded and for just a moment his thoughts were filled with Suzanna. They had always seemed to know what the other was thinking or about to say. "It's a twin thing," they'd say to their friends. He'd felt gutted since her death, as if half his soul had been stolen and would never be returned.

"And where were you on the night that Max was murdered?" Her question made the here and now slam back into him.

But, God, she was attractive. Today she was clad in a pair of black jeans that hugged her legs and a red tank top that matched her red heels and hinted at a bit of cleavage.

How many men had lost themselves in the depths of her blue eyes or in the utter charm of her smile and spilled their guts? She smelled of something citrusy with mysterious spices that were incredibly evocative.

"Where were you when Max was murdered?" she asked again.

He mentally shook himself and focused on the question, not on how sexy he found her. "I was at Doug's Tavern in a meeting with the mayor, half a dozen city councilmen and some local architects. We were discussing the renovation and renewal project going on downtown. Then I came back here and slept."

"Alone?"

He gave a curt nod. "Yes, I was alone." He knew Max's time of death was sometime between midnight and two in the morning. And that meant he had no real alibi for the time of the murder. He'd been questioned briefly by the police the day after the murder, but he hadn't heard anything more from the authorities.

"And how did you learn about Max's murder?"

"I read it in the newspaper like most of the people in Kansas City."

"Would you like to tell me something about your sister?" Her features radiated a soft sympathy.

Oh, he'd love to talk about his sister…about the loving, wonderfully magical woman she had been. But it would cheapen Suzanna to talk about her to this stranger who was only looking for her next scoop.

"No," he answered simply. "Why are you here talking to me?"

"When Max Clinton was murdered, and a V was carved in his forehead, I knew he was a fourth victim of this particular killer. The police tried to keep the V out of the new reports from the very beginning, but somebody leaked it to the press."

He looked at her in surprise. "How do you know that?"

"I have a friend on the police force," she replied.

"You mean you have a snitch."

"Friend…snitch…whatever you want to call him, he occasionally gives me a little inside information that keeps me up to date with what's going on with the crime in Kansas City. I also heard there's going to be a news conference tomorrow and the police are going to ask the community for their help in catching this person."

Interesting. Jake would definitely like to know what was going on in the investigation into the Vigilante Killer, and Monica Wright just might make an interesting partner of sorts.

"You still haven't told me what, specifically, you want from me?" he said.

"Initially I thought you would make a good human interest story for my podcast, but then I got a tip about you and the three other men attending the Northland Survivor Group."

"Who was your source for that?" he asked.

She smiled and her eyes gleamed with both intelligence and wit. "I don't give up the name of my sources. So do you know Nick Simon, Troy Anderson and Matt Harrison?"

"I do. You're right, we all attended meetings

there around the same time, but what does that have to do with anything?"

"So it's just an odd coincidence that the killer has gone after the men who ruined all your lives?" She shook her head and once again her eyes shone with keen intelligence. "I'm sorry, but I don't believe in those kinds of coincidences. The killer seems to have a connection to the survivor group, and that means you might know him." She leaned forward. "If you know something about the killer, then please tell me."

"Why should I tell you anything?" he countered. "I don't even know you. You're just somebody who showed up unannounced on my doorstep."

"So why did you invite me?" she countered.

"Because you caught my interest when you mentioned the survivor group and the other men."

"Have you ever seen my podcast?"

He took another sip of his drink before replying. "I've caught it a couple of times."

"Then you should know I'm good at what I do. I dig into investigations and there's nobody in this city who wants to identify this killer more than me. I want this… I need this to prove to everyone that I'm here to stay, that what I do with my podcast is a real job." Her cheeks flushed pink, as if she hadn't meant to say so much. She leaned back.

He studied her for a long moment. "Then we

both want the same thing. I want this killer caught and I intend to bring him down. He's obviously unhinged and enjoys killing, and I don't see him stopping anytime soon."

She frowned, the gesture doing nothing to detract from her attractiveness. "He's smart and he's thorough. He hasn't left a single clue behind for the police to work with. They are frustrated by their lack of leads. Right now he's killing what most of society would deem bad guys, but that still makes him a murderer."

"I totally agree."

She gazed at him for a long moment. "What's your story? You're a successful, award-winning architect. What would make you want to suddenly become a killer-hunter?"

He certainly wasn't ready to trust her with the details of the murder pact six men had made in the woods behind an abandoned baseball field.

To give the information he had to anyone presented a huge risk, not only to himself but also to the four other innocent men in the group. He felt responsible for the birth of the Vigilante Killer and he had to somehow figure out how to point a finger for the police. But first, he had to see which one of the remaining two men was the guilty one. And the only way to do that was to do some investigating of his own.

"Let's just say I feel a moral obligation to go after him," he finally replied.

She narrowed her eyes. "So you do know something."

"I might," he admitted.

Her eyes lit with an obvious hunger, and he momentarily wondered what it would feel like if her eyes lit up like that when she looked at him as a man and not just as a source for a big story.

"If we both want the same thing then there's no reason why we couldn't partner up. I can share with you all the information I have and you could share with me."

The offer surprised him. He had to admit there was a part of him that had longed to talk about what he knew with somebody. But he'd never dreamed he'd share any of this with anyone, especially not with an ambitious reporter.

"I need some time to think about it," he finally said.

"How much time?"

"I don't know…give me twenty-four hours." He wanted to stop the Vigilante Killer, but he'd certainly never thought about having a partner who may have some resources to help him achieve that goal.

She checked her wristwatch and then stood.

"Okay, twenty-four hours it is. I've got to get home now to do my podcast."

He rose as well. "I hope nothing we discussed here is in your podcast tonight," he said as they walked to his front door.

"Contrary to what you believe about me, I know how to keep secrets. How can I catch up with you tomorrow?"

"How about you have dinner with me at D'Angelo's. Do you know where it is?" Even as he asked the question he wondered what in the hell he was doing.

"I do. What time is good for you?"

"Shall we say around six?"

She nodded and then smiled. "I'm looking forward to it."

"Tell Wally and Warren I said hi."

Her smile turned slightly sheepish. "Will do. I'll see you tomorrow." With that she turned and hurried out to her car.

He watched until she pulled out of his driveway and then he closed and locked his front door. His brain spun wildly as he returned to his recliner and picked up what was left of his drink.

What in the hell was he doing even thinking about sharing what he knew with her? And he'd definitely lost his mind in inviting her out to dinner.

If he was going to work with her in any way,

it would be a fine line he'd have to walk to make sure he didn't incriminate himself or the others. But she was a wild card in this whole mess and he knew she wasn't going to stop digging. At least if he worked with her he might be able to guide her investigation on a path he wanted to keep it on.

Still, he had to remember that she would throw him under the bus in a minute to get her story.

It was just after five thirty when Monica angled her car into a parking place down the street from D'Angelo's Restaurant. It was a popular place to dine with great Italian food and reasonable prices, but on a Sunday evening there would be fewer diners.

She'd come away from Jake's house last night with the gut-burning certainty that he had some knowledge that would help move the investigation forward.

There had been shadows in his deep green eyes that had whispered of secrets, secrets she definitely wanted him to share with her.

Had she worn her royal blue cold-shoulder blouse tonight because she'd had several people tell her she looked sexy in it? Had she decided to wear her black skinny jeans because she knew they hugged her thin but shapely legs? Was it all in an effort to use her womanly wiles on him?

Maybe, but she had to admit part of it was for him to see Monica Wright not just as a sharp investigative reporter, but also as a desirable woman.

Which was completely ridiculous. The very last thing she wanted in her life was a relationship that would suck time and energy away from her work, but there were times she was lonely. It was really rather silly, but something about talking to Jake the evening before had made her think about her loneliness.

Maybe it was because from the moment she had met him, butterflies had danced in her stomach. And she hadn't felt butterflies about any man in a very long time.

She raised a finger to her mouth and then dropped her hand back to the steering wheel. She was desperately trying to stop chewing her nails. It was hard to have pretty nails when you gnawed them ragged. Instead she now clicked them against her steering wheel as her thoughts continued to cascade in her head.

It's about the story, stupid. This had been her mantra for the last five years, when she had really gotten serious about what she wanted to do. The advertising on her podcast paid her bills, but she wanted more than just financial security. She wanted respect. And identifying the Vigilante

Killer and being responsible for his arrest would gain her that respect.

This was the first case where she didn't just want to report the facts; rather, she wanted to make the facts. She wanted to hunt the killer.

It was definitely interesting to her that Jake had wanted nothing more than to kick her off his property until she'd mentioned the three other men and the Northland Survivor Group. He had suddenly become quite amenable after that.

He'd started out just being a possible human-interest story. Janet McCall's phone call had changed all that. Talking to him last night had also changed that. He was so much more than a human-interest story. She had a feeling he might be the key to discovering the identity of the killer.

Her clicking fingernails stopped and she sat up straighter in her seat as Jake's car pulled into a parking space on the opposite side of the street.

The butterflies took flight again in her stomach as he got out of the car and headed inside the restaurant. His black slacks fit perfectly on his slim hips and long legs, and he also wore a dark green short-sleeved shirt she knew would perfectly match his eyes.

She waited five minutes and then, ignoring the dancing butterflies, she got out of her car and headed for the restaurant's front door.

It was cool and semi-dark inside. Scents of garlic and onion and rich Italian spices filled the air, and soft music played overhead. A pretty, young hostess greeted her. "Hi, is there just one this evening?"

"No, I'm meeting somebody here. Jake Lamont?"

The hostess smiled again. "Oh yes, if you'll follow me."

The hostess guided her through the main dining room and into a smaller private room with a table for two.

Jake stood as they entered, and for just a brief moment she wondered what it would be like if he had gotten the private room because he wanted to know her hopes and dreams…because he wanted to spend time gazing into her eyes and whispering sweet nothings in her ear.

Of course nothing could be further from the truth. He'd gotten the private dining room because they had things to discuss, things like murder and a serial killer working in her hometown.

"This is nice," she said once the hostess was gone and the two of them were seated at the table.

"I figured it would be good to meet in a neutral place to have this discussion," he replied. "But how about we eat first and then talk about the main issue."

"That works for me," she agreed.

He gestured toward the menu. "I've already decided what I want," he said.

She opened the menu but as she read the offerings, she was acutely aware of his gaze on her. She made her decision, closed the menu and met his gaze.

He looked away and for a moment an awkward silence ensued. Thankfully a waitress entered the room and broke the silence.

She served them water and a mini loaf of garlic bread and whipped butter. She took both their drink and meal orders, and then left the room once again.

"How was your day?" he asked when they were alone again.

She looked at him in surprise. She couldn't remember the last time anyone had inquired about her day. "Do you really want to know or are you just being polite?" she asked.

"I'd really like to know," he replied.

"My morning was rough. Most of them are rough. I'm not a morning person and everything that can go wrong in a day usually happens then. Yesterday my coffee machine quit working. I bought a new one and this morning I went to make coffee and realized I was out of pods."

A corner of his mouth lifted. "Sounds disastrous."

"Oh, trust me. It was. I am not a happy camper without my morning coffee. Anyway, the rest of my day was good. I'm working on several stories right now and things are coming together nicely on them. How did your day go?"

"It was quiet. I watched a little television and then sketched for a while. I hate Sundays, when the job site is closed down and there's nothing much for me to do."

"Do you have family here in town?"

"I don't have family anywhere," he replied. "My parents are gone and it was just Suzanna and me. What about you? Do you have family here?"

"My mother died when I was eight, but I have my father and two older, overachieving sisters. Addie and Elizabeth are the apples of his eyes."

"Which implies that you aren't?" He raised a dark brow.

"I've been his disappointment for years," she replied, and fought against a hurtful hitch in her heart.

Their conversation was interrupted by the arrival of their meals. He'd ordered the spaghetti and meatballs while she had opted for cheese ravioli. "Oh my gosh, this looks yummy."

"Can I cut you off some bread?"

"Yes, please."

He cut her a piece. "Butter?"

"Definitely," she replied.

He slathered the bread with butter and then handed it to her. As their fingertips touched, the butterflies in her stomach flew once again. Good Lord, what was wrong with her?

"I think Italian food is my favorite type of food," he said as he cut himself a piece of the bread.

"Italian is good, but Mexican is my very favorite," she replied. "There's nothing better than chips and salsa and cheese enchiladas."

For a few minutes they were quiet as they focused on their meal. On the one hand, Monica wanted to hurry up and eat so they could get to the conversation she wanted to have with him. On the other hand, there was a small part of her that wanted the meal to go slow so she could somehow pretend this was a normal first date between a man and a woman who were interested in each other.

Jeez, once again she wondered what was wrong with her. All she wanted from Jake Lamont was any information he might have about the Vigilante Killer. She wanted her big story, and that was it.

She had to stay focused and not get caught up in his beautiful green eyes with their thick dark lashes and the sexy slide of his lips curving into a smile. Okay, she found him vastly attractive, but she needed to maintain her emotional distance from him. She had to remember that he was nothing more than a means to an end.

"So, why news?" he asked as they continued to eat.

She shrugged. "Why architecture?"

"I loved the way buildings looked. I always knew I wanted to design amazing buildings."

"And I was always fascinated with the women reporters on the news. I studied them and tried to figure out what made them popular. I always knew I wanted to be an investigative reporter and really dig into the stories I thought impacted the Kansas City area."

"Why not work for one of the big networks?" He cut himself off another piece of the bread.

"It's a whole new world. More and more people are getting their news from alternative sources and I wanted to be one of those alternative sources." She offered him a smile. "Besides, I like being my own boss. I don't always play well with others."

He raised a dark brow once again. "Ah, good to know, especially when you want to partner up with me."

"I'll let you in on a little secret about me…if you're working with me, then I'll be the most loyal person in the whole world to you."

"Now all I have to do is believe you."

"Trust me, you can believe me," she said fervently. Their gazes locked for a long moment. She couldn't tell if he believed her or not, but what she'd told him was the honest-to-goodness truth.

It was she who broke the gaze, finding it suddenly too probing…too intimate. "I'd go to prison before I'd ever give up the name of a source. Despite my ambition, I like to think I have a big streak of integrity inside me."

"Integrity is a good thing to have," he replied.

They finished their meals and he pushed his empty plate aside. "How about some dessert with coffee? I never miss a chance to have something sweet to finish off a meal."

She flashed him a cheeky grin. "Nothing I like better than chocolate and murder. Let's get to it then."

HE HAD TAKEN the last twenty-four hours to think about what he was going to tell Monica. Could he trust her? Even though he had absolutely no reason to, his gut instinct was that he could. After all, they both wanted the same thing.

Or maybe it was because he desperately wanted to trust her. He needed somebody like her to know what had taken place in the woods that night…in case something happened to him. If she ran directly to the cops with what he told her and he was arrested, well, maybe that was okay as well. Maybe it was exactly what he deserved.

He ordered tiramisu and she opted for chocolate lava cake. They both ordered coffee, and once they'd been served and were alone again, he studied her closely.

Was he deciding to trust her because she looked amazing in the sexy blue blouse that bared her slender shoulders and matched her eyes? Was he weakened by the fact that when she smiled at him a crazy warmth filled him? No, he wasn't that stupid. This was far too important to make that kind of a mistake.

It was the directness of her gaze and the honesty, and yes, integrity he sensed in her that finally made up his mind to confide what he could to her. Besides, he needed an insurance policy so that if something did happen to him she could take the information he gave her to the police and hopefully get the killer behind bars.

"Let's just assume there were six angry men," he began. "They had all suffered the loss of a loved one by bad men. Not only that, but due to jury nullification and technical glitches and other problems in the judicial system, those bad men all got away with their crimes."

He stared down into his coffee as he remembered the killing rage and grief that had made him half-crazed after Suzanna's murder. His rage had been further fired by the fact that Max Clinton walked away a free man.

He gazed back at her. "Anyway, these six men all found themselves at the Northland Survivor Group. They were all looking for ways to deal with their emotions. They were hoping to learn some new coping skills or something to help them with their overwhelming pain."

"And did they find what they needed?" she asked softly.

"No, they didn't. They met several times for drinks after the meetings, talking about their grief and their rage at the system, but they found no relief until they decided to hatch a plan."

Once again he paused, this time to take a drink of his coffee and eat a bite of his dessert. It was tasteless and he knew it was because his mouth was filled with the taste of grief and shame and the enormous bitterness of deep guilt.

He still couldn't believe he'd actually been a part of the plot they had all come up with on that crazy night. It had definitely been a moment of temporary insanity.

"Anyway," he continued, "the more these men all got together, the greater their anger grew." A knot expanded and twisted tight in his chest. "And then one night they all met in the woods next to an old abandoned baseball field. It was on that night they came up with a stupid plan."

This was the part where he had to get a little inventive in order to protect not only himself but the other men who had come up with what now was a horrendous plot. He definitely believed that one of them was the killer, but that meant he and four others were innocent.

"A stupid plan?" She put her fork down and stared at him intently.

He was afraid to tell, but there was also a part of him that wanted to spill his guts to her about everything…a part of him that needed to get this burden off his chest.

"You have to remember that we were all crazy with grief," he said, as if that somehow mitigated what they'd planned to get the justice they all wanted.

"This is a judgement-free zone," she replied.

He released a deep sigh. "To be honest, I don't know for sure who came up with the idea, but it was planned that we would each kill another man's killer. For instance, I'd kill the man who murdered Nick Simon's wife. Nick would kill the man who beat Matt Harrison's mother to death, and so on."

He paused and watched her features carefully, seeking a sign of shock and revulsion. But none was there. All he saw was open curiosity.

"Looking back at that meeting in the woods, it seems like a bad dream, not something that really happened. But it did." He paused and drew a deep breath. "And we all walked away from that meeting thinking we were going to act on that plan. But when it came right down to it, I would have never been able to kill a man, no matter what heinous crimes he'd committed, and I believe the others were just like me. Don't get me wrong, the idea of the murder pact was appealing, but I didn't believe any of it would really happen."

The waitress's entering the room with a coffee-pot interrupted the conversation. She topped off their coffee, and he handed her his charge card and then once again she left the room.

"Anyway," he continued, "I didn't believe any of it was really going to happen until the first man was killed." His chest tightened with tension as he remembered reading about the murder in the paper.

"Brian McDowell," she said. "He's the man who beat Matt Harrison's mother to death."

"Right. Nick Simon was supposed to kill him, but Nick didn't kill him, and that's when I believe the Vigilante Killer was born."

"So, you believe the Vigilante Killer is one of four men?"

"I don't believe that any of the men who got

their so-called justice through the Vigilante Killer is guilty. I think the killer is one of the last two men. He's either Clay Rogers or Adam Kincaid."

"What are you going to do about it?" Her eyes were lit with an eagerness that made him second-guess his crazy decision to trust her.

Still, he figured in for a penny, in for a pound. "I've been thinking about it since Max Clinton was murdered." An idea had been whirling around in his head since the morning he'd read about Max's death in the paper. "I know all the murders have happened between midnight and two in the morning, so I figure the only way to identify the killer is to watch these two men during those hours until one of them makes a move."

"And then what?"

"Once I know for sure who the killer is, then I'll take him down. Hopefully I can subdue him and then contact the police. I need to get him behind bars." He frowned. "I think this person likes to kill, Monica. And the carving in the foreheads of his victims speaks of a bloodlust that is absolutely disgusting."

"I completely agree. There's only one thing I ask. Once we identify the killer, I want time to break the story before anyone else gets it," she replied. Her eyes gleamed brightly.

He didn't miss her use of "we" in her sentence.

"I can give you that," he replied. "But this is something I need to do for myself and there's no reason for you to get involved in this at all. I'll let you know when I have confirmation on who the killer is and you'll have your story."

"But I am involving myself. I want to be a part of this. Jake, I want to do the surveillance with you," she protested.

There was one more interruption by the waitress to bring back his receipt and credit card.

"Monica, this could be dangerous," he said once they were alone again. "Whoever the killer is, the last thing he wants is to get caught. He's ruthless."

"I know that, but think about it—two people are better than one. We could do surveillance from your car one night and then from mine the next night to make sure nobody gets suspicious. We can wake each other up if we drift off to sleep."

He shook his head. "I just don't think it's a good idea. One of the reasons I told you all this is that I want somebody else to know in case something happens to me."

"Why would something happen to you?"

"I don't know, but if this man is as ruthless as I believe him to be, then all the rest of us in the pact are loose ends. If he catches wind that I'm hunting him, then there's no question he'll come after me."

"I still want to be a part of this. I have the two

names of the men you think it might be. I'll just conduct my own surveillance if I'm not doing it with you." Her chin shot up a notch and her eyes held a definite challenge.

"Don't make me regret I told you all this," he said. Damn, he should have never given her the names of the two men he suspected. That had been careless of him.

"Then don't try to cut me out of the action," she replied. She reached out and covered his hand with hers, the unexpected pleasant touch sparking an electric jolt in him. "Please, Jake. Don't try to shut me out of this." She pulled her hand back. "Why don't I plan on being at your house tomorrow night at eleven thirty and we can get started."

"Okay," he finally relented. The last thing he wanted was for her to go off all half-cocked and either screw things up or get herself killed. He already had enough guilt in his heart to last a lifetime. "Are you ready to get out of here?"

"I am," she agreed.

He'd already taken care of the tab, so they left the private room, walked through the main dining area and then stepped out into the hot night air.

"Hey, bitch," a deep voice shouted from behind them.

They both turned and Jake got a quick look at a dark-haired scruffy-looking man standing on the sidewalk. The man raised his hand and threw something.

Jake grabbed her to his chest and whirled her around to protect her as a beer bottle shattered on the sidewalk next to them.

"What the hell?" With Monica behind him he turned to confront the man. But he was gone, the sound of his running feet on the pavement letting Jake know the man was retreating. A few moments later a car door slammed in the distance and then a car roared by them.

"Bitch!" the man yelled out of the window as he drove by.

"What was that all about?" he turned and asked Monica.

"That was Larry Albright. He's a local contractor I did an exposé on a couple of days ago. He had ripped off dozens of homeowners, mostly elderly people, by telling them they needed new roofs. He then not only overcharged them but also used substandard materials. Needless to say, he's not happy with my reporting."

"What's he doing? Stalking you?" Jake asked in alarm.

"Apparently that's what he did tonight."

"Have you called the police?"

"No, I don't think he's a real threat to me. And in any case, he's been charged with half a dozen

crimes and he was released on his own recogni-
zance. He knows one phone call to the police from
me and he'll wind up in jail to await his trial. He's
just blowing off some steam. And now, thank you
for dinner, and I'll see you tomorrow night."

He watched as she walked to her car. She looked
gorgeous with the last gasp of sunlight playing in
her dark hair. She walked with a sexy confidence
despite the height of her heels.

Still, no matter how attractive he found her, no
matter how eager she was or how much he im-
plicitly trusted her, he couldn't help but feel this
whole situation just might have disaster written
all over it.

Chapter Three

"Join me again tomorrow night for part two of 'Gang Violence in Kansas City.' And as always, make sure you're getting the right news with Monica Wright."

She clicked off her microphone and camera and scooted away from the desk. This spare room in her house was her "newsroom." She had her high-dollar microphone, camera and computer. There were three televisions tuned to news stations. She also had a red, white and blue backdrop that looked professional.

Tonight she'd started a six-part investigative report on the growing gang activities in the area. Each weekend there were more shootings and more deaths, mostly happening in the south of the downtown area.

She'd been thrilled to snag an interview with a self-proclaimed gangbanger who, surprisingly, was an intelligent young man who had chosen a life as a dope dealer because he he'd seen no other future for himself.

A life of poverty and a lack of opportunity had stolen his hopes and dreams of a different kind of future. It had ended up being a compelling piece that she was proud of, but it was her plans for later that night that had her pumped up and excited.

Tonight she and Jake would begin their quest to catch a killer. A shiver of excitement worked up her spine as she changed from her business attire to a short-sleeved black blouse and black jeans.

There was no question that she'd been shocked the night before when he'd told her about the plan the six men had come up with. She'd been shocked and yet oddly humbled that he had decided to trust her enough to give her that information.

If she was a different kind of woman, a different kind of reporter, she could have taken what he'd told her and run with a sensational story of six bloodthirsty men on a quest for murder.

She was far more interested in the end game of getting a killer off the streets and in jail. Besides, she found it hard to believe that anyone could find six men, no matter how angry or how much they were grieving, who would actually commit cold-blooded murder.

The really big story would be identifying that

killer and getting him arrested. That's what she wanted: the final story of a killer's end.

She especially didn't think Jake Lamont was the kind of a man who could murder another human being. Call it women's intuition or her hope that she was a good judge of character, but she didn't believe Jake Lamont had it in him to kill anyone no matter how crazy he'd been with grief and rage. Otherwise why would he have told her his story? Of course, she could always be wrong about him. Time would tell.

At eleven she packed some snacks in her purse, grabbed a small cooler that held several cold drinks and then went out to her car. As she walked in the darkness toward where her car was parked in the driveway, she kept an eye out for anyone else in the area.

Larry Albright's attack the night before had shaken her up more than just a little bit. She'd never had anyone she'd reported on come after her. What she'd told Jake was true—she didn't see him as a real threat—but still he'd surprised her by stalking her to the restaurant and throwing that bottle. She hoped that was the end of him bothering her.

She reached her car and settled in, confident there was nobody watching her. Once she pulled out and got on the road, she kept her gaze on the rearview mirror for several miles, but didn't see anyone following her.

She'd spent much of her day researching what she could find out about the five other men Jake had named as belonging to the group.

There had been two engagement announcements. Both Nick Simon and Troy Anderson had gotten engaged in the last month. She couldn't find much information about any of the other men, but she assumed Jake would fill her in about them tonight.

When she was about five miles from his house a new kind of excitement filled her. There was no question she found Jake attractive. She'd met a lot of attractive men in the past, had even dated a couple, but she had never allowed herself to get too close or emotionally involved.

It's about the story, stupid, she reminded herself. And over the next couple of nights hopefully she could get the information she needed to break the biggest story of her career.

Light spilled out of Jake's bay window. She parked in his driveway and then grabbed her things and headed for his front door. He answered on her first knock. He wore a pair of black jeans, a black T-shirt and a deep frown.

"I was hoping you'd have changed your mind about coming with me," he said.

"No way," she replied firmly.

"I still think this is a bad idea." His frown deepened.

"I don't know why," she replied. "Starsky needed his Hutch, Batman needed his Robin. Heck, even Turner needed his Hooch."

The corner of his lower lip curled up. "Hooch? Really?"

"Hey, you never know when you might need a big, slobbering dog. Woof."

His lips completed a full smile and then he shook his head. "I have a feeling this might be a long night."

She laughed. "Well, let's get this party started."

Minutes later they were in his car and headed to Clay Rogers's house. "Tell me about Clay," she said as she tried to ignore the very pleasant spicy scent of Jake's cologne.

"He works the financials at a car dealership. His girlfriend went out for a run one night and never came back. Her body was found the next day in a field. She'd been raped and strangled."

"That's tragic," she replied, unable to even comprehend the kind of pain such an event would cause in a loved one.

"Yeah, what's even more tragic is they found the killer by checking out video in the area. His name is Charlie Cohen. He was seen following her in his car and then parking and getting out of his car and chasing after her."

"Let me guess, for some reason he walked free."

Jake nodded. In the dim lighting from the dashboard his handsome features appeared grim. "He had a high-dollar lawyer who argued Charlie had just wanted her to make a phone call for him because he had a flat tire. There was no actual footage of him actually grabbing her, and the jury hung. The prosecutor didn't feel like he had the evidence to retry."

She fought the impulse to touch him, to reach over and stroke the tension out of his shoulders. "So you all not only felt the pain of your own loss, but it sounds like you shared each other's pain as well."

"We did." He released a deep sigh and some of the tension left him. "Clay was the youngest of all of us, and I liked him, but if he is the Vigilante Killer, then he needs to be stopped."

"And that's why we're in a car in the middle of the night," she replied.

They fell silent as they continued to drive the dark streets to Clay's house. They had no idea when the killer would strike again, but Monica had a feeling it wouldn't be too long.

She believed Jake was right. This person liked what he was doing. It took a sick mind-set to slit somebody's throat, but that's how this man was killing his victims. And what was he going to do when he'd taken care of all the men who had wronged the six of them? Would he then move on to murder other people?

She sat up straighter in the seat as Jake slowed the car. He turned onto a tree-lined street. The houses were modest and most of them were completely dark at this time of night.

Jake pulled up to the curb and stopped the car. He doused his headlights and cut the engine. "That's Clay's house," he said, and pointed to the house on the opposite side of the street from where they were parked.

It was a small ranch house with a neat and tidy yard. It, too, was dark, but if he was the killer, it was possible lights could come on at any minute and he would leave the house with murder in mind.

"Might as well get comfortable," he said. He unfastened his seat belt and moved his seat back to give himself more legroom.

She did the same and then opened her purse. "Want some licorice?"

"No, thanks."

"What about some corn chips or spice drops or dried apple slices?"

He turned in the seat to look at her, his features barely discernible in the faint illumination from a nearby streetlight. "Do you really have all those snacks in your purse?"

"Ah, this isn't an ordinary purse tonight. It's a surveillance survivor kit. Not only do I have snacks, but I've also got antibiotic cream and bandage strips, a bottle of pain reliever and ChapStick just to name a few things."

"So I can eat spice drops while you bandage up a wound and make sure my lips don't get chapped," he replied.

"Exactly. See, this is why you need me with you for surveillance."

"I've got a surveillance kit, too," he said.

"Really? What do you have?"

"A flashlight and a gun."

His words instantly sobered her. This wasn't just two people sitting in a car in the middle of the night laughing and eating junk food. This was a potentially dangerous situation. If the murderer saw them watching him, she had a feeling he wouldn't hesitate to kill them.

"You do realize this could take more than a night or two," he said, breaking into her frightening thoughts.

"I know that, but I don't think it's going to be too long before he strikes again," she replied.

"I agree." He stared past her and toward the

house. "It's also possible we're sitting on the wrong man. I hope it isn't Clay."

"Tell me about the other man... Adam Kincaid."

"Adam's wife was murdered after she withdrew two hundred dollars from an ATM. A drug addict pulled her out of the car and beat her for the money. She might have survived, but he slammed her head into the pavement so hard it killed her. Before it went to trial, the perp was offered immunity in order to bring down a drug ring operating in the city."

"My God, I can't believe how badly the justice system let you all down," she replied.

"Thank God cases like ours don't happen every day and for the most part justice prevails."

"Still, it's horrible how the six of you saw no justice," she replied. "It must have been incredibly difficult for you to know Max was still walking around free after he murdered your sister."

"It was difficult," he admitted.

Once again she fought the impulse to reach out and touch him. She could understand the grief and rage that all these men felt.

He grabbed a flashlight from the console. "I need to get out and check to make sure his car is in the garage. Otherwise he could already be gone, and we wouldn't know we were sitting on an empty house."

"No," she exclaimed, reaching out and grabbing hold of his arm. "I don't want you to do that. It's too dangerous."

"How dangerous could it be for me to just take a peek into the garage?" he asked.

"Lights could flash on and an alarm could sound. Guard dogs could suddenly appear...dogs with big sharp teeth and trained to kill."

He gently pulled his arm out of her grasp. "If that happens, we implement plan B."

"And what's plan B?" she asked.

"You duck down and I run like hell."

HE GOT OUT of the car as silently as possible and for a moment remained in place and stared at Clay's house. Around him the night was silent other than the insects that clicked and whirred their normal night songs. The three-quarter moon overhead helped him see clearly.

But that also meant the moonlight might help somebody else see him. He looked at all the other homes, assured by the darkness within each one. Hopefully the occupants were all soundly sleeping and would never know that he had been here.

He didn't need his flashlight as he raced across the street and toward the doors of the two-car garage, which each held a small window. His heart beat a steady rhythm and the scent of freshly mowed grass filled his nose.

He reached the garage doors. A bright light suddenly bathed the area in front of the garage. His heart stopped. Was an alarm now ringing someplace inside the house? He took a moment to peek into one of the windows and then he took off running.

His heart beat so hard it felt as if it was going to burst right out of his chest. He didn't look back. He just ran. When he was three doors down from Clay's place, he spied a large tree and ducked behind it.

He drew in several long, deep breaths in an attempt to slow his heartbeat. Was this whole plan an act of stupidity? Maybe, but it was the only way he knew to identify the killer. And he felt morally responsible to do so.

Several minutes passed and the light over Clay's garage went off. There was no indication that anyone on the inside of the house had been roused out of sleep, no sign of anyone rushing to check things out.

A simple motion detector light, that's what Jake bet it was. Not an alarm or anything like that, just a light that came on to warn people away. A meandering cat or a dog could have set it off.

He waited another couple of minutes and then,

assured that nothing more was going to happen, he raced back across the street and headed to his car.

Monica was hunkered down half on the floor, her eyes huge as he slid back inside. "Are we safe?" she asked worriedly.

"We're safe. You can get up now."

She settled back in the seat and released a deep sigh. "That was a little bit scary."

"I warned you this could get a little scary. Are you ready to let me do this by myself? I could still keep you informed when I manage to identify the killer."

"No way," she replied. "We're partners in this until the very end."

He'd half hoped that she would insist he take her back to her car and that she'd allow him to do this by himself. She was a bit of a distraction with her citrusy-spicy scent eddying in the air. He was far too conscious of her, not as a partner, but as a woman…a very desirable woman.

For the past two years he'd kept himself isolated. He'd shunned any kind of a social life and had focused only on his work. He would remain alone forever, as penance for the events that had unfolded on the night his sister was murdered.

Monica was the first woman in the last couple of years to tempt him just a little bit. He couldn't help but notice her petite but perfectly proportioned body. Her skin looked soft and touchable, and he liked the way her eyes sparkled and the shape of her mouth.

But more than his physical attraction to her was the fact that he was somehow drawn to the energy that wafted from her. It was an energy that spoke of curiosity and intelligence and a real zest for living that reminded him of what life had been like for him before Suzanna's murder.

Thankfully, she obviously saw him only as a means to an end, so she wouldn't be too much of a temptation for him. He just wanted to get the Vigilante Killer before he struck again.

"Did you see if his car was in the garage?" she now asked.

"It was there."

"I've got to admit, I was terrified for you when those lights went on."

"I was a little bit scared for myself," he admitted. "Thank goodness it was just a motion detector and there were no guard dogs with big, scary teeth."

He settled back in his seat and stared down the road. They were betting that the killer would adhere to the timeline he'd set up with the four previous murders. It was close to midnight now, and they'd remain in place until just after two and then head back to his house.

"This is going to play hell with our daily schedules," he said.

"I really don't have much of a regular schedule," she replied. "As long as I take several hours to research and do my homework for the podcast each night, then I can sleep until noon if I want to."

"I don't have that luxury right now. We're in the middle of putting up a high-rise building and I like to be on-site every day to work with the builder."

"Whatever you do, don't go up in a high-rise and then get sleepy and fall off."

He smiled. "Trust me, I always wear a safety belt when I go up high. Generally, I don't do crazy things."

"Sitting in a car in the middle of the night to try to catch a serial killer…you don't consider this crazy?" Her tone was teasing.

"Oh, it's crazy all right, but I also feel like it's my duty. I don't believe anyone else is trying to stop him and we both know so far he hasn't made a mistake to help the police in their investigation."

She reached over and placed her hand on his forearm. Her fingers were warm and soft, and he fought the need to overreact to the touch and jerk his arm away.

"Jake, I find what you're doing right now to be quite admirable."

"I'm the last person anyone should admire,"

he scoffed, grateful when she removed her hand from him.

The car was suddenly too warm. He started the engine and turned the air conditioner on high. He felt her gaze lingering on him, but he didn't turn his head to look at her.

"Jake, I have a feeling this man would have eventually killed with or without anyone else's involvement. He's playing God and from all indications he likes it."

"That's why he needs to be stopped. I'm afraid that after he kills all the men who hurt us, he'll move on to killing other people. Not all people charged with a crime are guilty and there's no way of knowing who he might move on to next."

Strange, he was far more comfortable talking murder with her than talking about anything else. He didn't want to make small talk with her. He didn't want to get to know her better. They were partners with a common goal, and that was it.

With the interior of the car sufficiently cooled off, he cut the engine.

"You told me both of your parents were gone. What happened to them?" she asked.

Apparently, she intended to make small talk. He sighed. He rarely thought of his parents, who had spent their lives making bad choices.

"They were both drug addicts from the time

Suzanna and I were four or five. Our father overdosed and died when we were eleven. Mom tried to clean up and pull it together, but she never managed it. She wound up overdosing and dying when we had just turned eighteen."

"Oh, wow. I'm so sorry," she replied.

"Thanks, but it was a long time ago." His childhood had been more than difficult, but he'd always believed it had made him strong, and it had bonded him and his sister together in a way that even went beyond their twin connection. They'd always had only each other to depend on.

"Tell me about your sisters and your father." Even though he didn't want to know too much about her, it seemed the proper thing to ask. In any case, he was grateful to keep the conversation off him and his miserable life.

She shifted positions in the seat and leaned closer to him. "My sisters are five and six years older than me. Addie is the eldest. She's married and has two daughters. She's also a nurse. Elizabeth is also married and has a little girl. She and her husband have their own law firm. At birth I was a disappointment to my father. I was supposed to be the boy he'd wanted."

"I'm sure that didn't change how much he loved you," Jake replied.

"I don't know, I always felt as if I had to work

extra hard to please him. Of course, my two sisters being overachieving Goody Two-shoes didn't help, and I did go through a couple of years of a little rebellion in high school."

Somehow this didn't surprise him about her. "How much of a rebellion?"

She grinned. "Not that bad. It was the usual teenage stuff. I blew off curfews and partied a little. More recently, Dad isn't exactly thrilled at my choice of careers. He thinks I'm just wasting my time and playing at a job. He doesn't understand that this is my passion and my chosen path."

For the next hour and a half they talked about their jobs. She told him about past stories she had run, including her investigation into gang activity, and he told her about the buildings he'd envisioned and had the pleasure to see through to completion.

He broke down and ate a handful of corn chips and they opened sodas that she had brought. There followed a good-natured argument about what was the best snack food. He liked salty and nutty, and she was definitely into sweet candy. She was so easy to talk to and he found himself completely relaxing with her company. They talked briefly about politics and agreed to disagree on some issues.

When two o'clock rolled around he was surprised by how quickly the time had gone by. "I think we're safe to get out of here now," he said. "If Clay is our man he would have already made a move if he was going to do anything tonight."

"I agree." She pulled her seat belt back around her, and he did the same and then started the car.

"Are you positive we just have to worry about one of these two men being the killer?" she asked as he headed back to his house.

He frowned thoughtfully. "I know without a doubt that the killer isn't Nick Simon or Troy Anderson. Both of those men were shaken up and freaked out when the men they were supposed to kill in the plan were killed. I also know those two men have moved on from this whole mess. They've found new love and want nothing to do with this. I'm not as sure in Matt Harrison's complete innocence. But I think the odds are the killer is either Clay or Adam."

"Are we back on Clay again tomorrow night?" She stifled a yawn with the back of her hand.

"I think we stick on him until something happens." A knot formed in Jake's chest. That something would be another man's murder unless he could stop it from happening. He prayed that he would be able to prevent the killer before another man was murdered.

They were quiet on the rest of the drive. "Will

you be okay to drive home?" he asked as he pulled into his driveway next to where her car was parked.

"I'll be fine," she assured him. "Same time tomorrow night?" she asked when they got out of the car.

"Unless you want to have dinner with me again. You mentioned that you like Mexican. How about I take you to El Chappo's?"

The moonlight bathed her face in a silvery light and her pleasure was obvious in the shine of her eyes and the curve of her lips. What in the hell was he thinking? What in the hell was he doing?

"I'd like that," she replied. "I've eaten there often and I love their food. Why don't I meet you there at around six?"

"Sounds good," he replied, even though he already wanted to take the invitation back.

Minutes later he watched as her car pulled away. He continued to watch until her lights disappeared and then he turned and went into his house.

Exhaustion filled him as he went into his bedroom and got ready for bed. It had been years since he'd had any kind of social interaction with anyone. He'd pushed away the friends he'd once had in his grief and rage.

They had been not only his friends, but Suzanna's as well. After her murder, seeing any of them had just been too painful.

Even though he and Monica had talked about nothing important, sharing conversation with her had felt good. It had stirred a hunger in him for more social talk, more time with her, making her even more of a temptation to him.

He shouldn't have asked her to eat with him again. He'd been foolish to invite her. He didn't want her to think that she was anything to him except part of his plan to catch a killer.

He'd liked being in her company and that wasn't good. She'd made him laugh, and there was no place in his life for laughter or fun. Max Clinton might have killed his sister, but Jake could never forgive himself for what he had done on that terrible night.

Chapter Four

Monica walked into El Chappo's and all her senses came alive. Rousing music played overhead and the walls were painted with colorful murals. The scents of tortillas and pork, of onions and enchilada sauce, rode the air.

Still, it was the sight of Jake sitting in a booth toward the back and waiting for her that really stirred her senses. He was such a hunk and she knew he'd smell wonderful. She liked the sound of his deep voice and especially enjoyed the rumble of his laughter.

She hated to admit it, but she'd been looking forward to having dinner with him all day long. She really hated to admit that she wanted to get to know him better.

She certainly hadn't expected to like him this much. She definitely needed him to break the biggest story of her career and of course that was her top priority. She just had to keep reminding herself of that. She wasn't ready for any kind of a relationship in her life. She needed all her energies and attention focused on her career.

"Good evening, Mr. Lamont," she said as she scooted into the booth seat across from his.

He smiled. "And good evening to you, Ms. Wright. I hope you brought your appetite."

"I'm starving." She reached for the basket of chips that sat in the center of the table. She grabbed one, dipped it in the bowl of hot sauce and popped it in her mouth. "Hmm, I love these things."

"They are addictive," he replied, and took one.

"You don't look too tired considering our overnight hours." In truth he looked amazing in a white short-sleeved shirt that complemented his glossy black hair and tanned skin.

"I managed to sneak in a nap this afternoon. What about you?"

"I slept in until almost eleven."

A waitress appeared at their table and took their drink orders. He got a soda and she opted for a strawberry daiquiri. Within minutes their drinks arrived and they placed their meal orders.

"Other than your nap, how was your day?" she asked once the waitress had left.

"It was good. Everything is going as scheduled on the new building and that's always a good thing. What about you?" He gazed at her with an intensity that threatened to steal her breath away. Under different circumstances it would be so easy to fall into the depths of his green eyes. Instead she grabbed another chip.

"It was okay. I ran some errands for my dad, because, you know, I don't have a real job." She couldn't help the touch of irritation that colored her voice. She crunched on the chip.

"Does that happen a lot?"

She nodded and swallowed. "More often than it should." She cast him a bright smile. "But all that will change once we complete our mission and I break the big story." She just knew then she'd get the respect from her father that she so longed for. That was her ultimate goal, to gain the love and respect from her father that she felt was missing in their relationship.

Despite the fact that a lot of the tables and booths were filled with diners, their meals arrived fairly quickly. He had ordered a pork-stuffed burrito and she had the cheese enchiladas. The servings were generous with sides of beans and rice.

"I could eat this kind of food every night for dinner," she said.

"I like it, but I'm not sure I'd want it every single night."

"So, what's your very favorite go-to food?"

"A good steak," he answered immediately.

"With a baked potato on the side. Now that I could eat almost every night."

"Butter and sour cream?"

He grinned at her. "Absolutely."

"Do you cook?" she asked him curiously. He couldn't be as perfect as he appeared.

"I can cook enough to stay alive," he replied. "But I certainly don't try anything too fancy. What about you?"

"Same, although I have to confess I prefer things that go from carton to microwave. It's always seemed like too big a hassle to cook for just one."

"I guess I should have asked you before, but you don't have a significant other?" Once again his eyes gazed at her intently, as if she were the most fascinating creature on the face of the earth.

"Yes, I have a significant other. It's my work. I can't remember the last time I went out on a date. That's why this is so nice. I mean, not that this is a real date or anything like that," she hurriedly added as a blush warmed her cheeks.

A small frown cut across his forehead. "No, this isn't a date. I don't date. I have no interest in having a relationship."

She wanted to ask him why he didn't want to have a relationship and why he'd invited her out to dinner. But his eyes suddenly appeared dark and shuttered, definitely not inviting any further questions on the topic.

"The one thing I do miss about having somebody in my life is that I have never really enjoyed eating alone," she finally said.

"I'm the same way and that's why I invited you out. I like a good meal, but it's even better if you have good company."

She smiled at him, grateful to see that the darkness that had been in his eyes momentarily was no longer there. "At least you consider me good company."

He returned her smile. "I can't imagine anyone considering you bad company."

A wave of warmth rushed through her. Jeez, what was wrong with her? Why did she want to get to know him better not as a story, but rather as a man? Why on earth did his smile, his intent gaze, make her heart skip a beat?

Loneliness. The word leaped into her head as she took another bite of her enchilada. Most of the time she kept busy enough she didn't have time to feel lonely.

But there were times, like when she saw a gorgeous sunset or thought of something funny or was just sitting alone in her living room, when a hollow wind of loneliness blew through her.

But she didn't intend to do anything about it.

Work first; there would always be time for a meaningful relationship after she had firmly established herself as a real success.

"I've refilled my surveillance bag for tonight," she said. "It now has corn nuts, potato chips and peanuts in it just for you."

Once again, he smiled. "You didn't have to do that. Did you also add some sweet stuff for you?"

"Definitely. I've been trying to quit chewing on my fingernails so I always have a bag of candy or packs of gum around the house."

"Is that helping?"

"Not really," she replied with frustration. "Most of the time I'm not even aware that I'm chewing on them."

"Haven't I heard something about putting hot sauce on your nails?"

She smiled. "Yes, I've heard that, too. The problem is I really love hot sauce so it wouldn't be a deterrent to me." She then frowned. "Is it just my imagination or is it getting a little smoky in here?"

"Now that you mention it, it is. They must have burned something in the kitchen."

"At least we know it isn't our dinners burning back there," she replied. "How is your burrito?"

"Absolutely delicious. What about your enchiladas?"

"I don't think I've ever had a bad cheese enchilada," she replied. "These are wonderful."

"What other kind of Mexican food do you like?"

"Anything on the menu," she replied with a laugh.

The words had just left her mouth when shouts could be heard coming from the kitchen. The mood of the dining room changed, quieting as the shouts from the back got louder and more frantic.

Several men wearing white aprons ran from the kitchen and into the dining room. "Fire," one of them yelled.

"*El incendio,*" another man shouted.

Panic ensued. Diners got out of their seats and pushed and shoved one another toward the entrance. There was an exit door two booths down from where she and Jake were seated. It was closer to the kitchen area, but easier than battling the rest of the people headed toward the main entrance.

They got up and Jake guided her toward that door. They weren't alone. Several others also headed in that direction.

The smoke grew thicker and heat radiated from the kitchen. They reached the door and Jake pushed on it. Apparently, it was locked, because it didn't open. However, the people behind them didn't seem to realize it. They pushed and shoved, getting more frantic.

As people pressed against her, panic crawled up the back of her throat. If the smoke and fire didn't get them, then they were going to be crushed to death in the panic.

"Let us out, man," a male voice yelled from behind them.

"It's locked," Jake yelled back. "The door is locked. We can't get out this way."

The heat from the kitchen grew more intense and still people pushed and shoved. Finally, the group at the exit door realized it was no way out and turned to head toward the main entrance. Jake threw his arm around her and pulled her close to his side as they also made for the entrance.

When they finally got outside two fire trucks, three police cars and several news vans had arrived. Everyone who had been in the building stood around, as if unsure what they should do.

Light bulbs flashed as photos were taken, microphones were shoved in people's faces and two ambulances roared into the parking lot with sirens screaming.

Jake pulled her closer and leaned into her. "Must be a slow news night," he murmured in her ear. "How about we get out of here."

"Sounds good to me," she replied.

They headed for their cars in the parking lot. The crowd began to break up as other people hurried toward their cars, too. She was grateful to see that none of the emergency vehicles had them blocked in.

"Well, that was exciting," she said as they reached her car.

"Definitely more excitement than I expected for a meal out," he agreed. He looked back at the restaurant and the emergency vehicles. "At least it looks like nobody got hurt."

"That's a good thing. For a minute there I thought I was going to be crushed by the crowd."

"I wouldn't have let that happen," he replied.

Warmth washed over her at his words. "Well, thank you, and I'll see you later tonight." She wanted to get home and write up a few notes on the fire to add to her podcast that night.

Besides, she needed just a little bit of distance from Jake. When he'd put his arm around her and pulled her close to his side, she'd wanted to stay there forever, and that was the last thing she needed from him.

"It's about the story, stupid," she muttered to herself as she drove away from the restaurant, where the fire was finally out.

JAKE AWAKENED THE next morning with a sense of dread. He'd tried not to think about this particular date for the past several days, but it slammed into him the moment he opened his eyes.

Two years ago today he had unlocked the door of Suzanna's house and had found her dead in her bedroom. The memory of that moment and the vision of his sister beaten and broken would remain with him forever. He would never forget the smell of death that had hung in the air.

At that moment he'd wanted nothing more than to run to the side of her bed. He'd wanted to gather her into his arms and weep…and scream. But he hadn't.

Even with wild grief clawing at his insides, someplace in the back of his mind, he'd known not to touch anything. He'd backed out of the bedroom and called the police. He'd then collapsed in the hallway and fallen apart.

It had been a kind policeman who had finally pulled him up and taken him out of the house. He'd sat in his patrol car with Jake while he screamed and sobbed.

When his tears had momentarily subsided, he'd managed to give a statement. The policeman had followed Jake in his car to ensure Jake got home safely.

He now finally roused himself out of the bed to shower and dress, and then he went out to retrieve his morning paper. He needed to keep busy today.

He needed to keep the memories at bay and not dwell on this horrible anniversary.

He made coffee and then sat at his table to read the paper. He was vaguely surprised to see on page two a report on the restaurant fire the night before. The brief article was accompanied by a photo of the restaurant and in the background, along with some of the other diners, Jake could be seen with his arm around Monica.

Once again last night they had spent several hours in front of Clay's place, where nothing had happened except he'd learned that Monica's favorite color was lavender, her favorite kind of music was old rock and roll and she made delicious throaty happy sounds when she ate gummy bears.

When he'd thrown his arm around her the night before to lead her out of the restaurant it hadn't been lost on him that she fit perfectly against him.

He was grateful to read the paper, drink his morning coffee, and then he needed to get to the job site where he didn't have to think about Monica's redolent scent. He didn't have to imagine her lavender bedroom or what it would be like to hear those throaty noises coming from her when his lips took hers.

The last thing he wanted to do was think about her and he certainly didn't want to dwell on memories of Suzanna and the last time he'd seen her.

It had been so terrible. He'd known she might be in trouble when noon rolled around and he hadn't heard from her. Not only had she not called him, but she hadn't answered any of his calls.

He'd driven to her house in a panic, knowing in his gut that something terrible had happened. And it had. Suzanna's death had been a defining moment that had changed his life forever.

He stuffed his memories deep inside and left the house at eight. He headed for the building site, hoping that talking to the men would keep his mind clear.

"Hey, Jake," Brett Cummings, the foreman on the job, greeted him as he got out of his car. "I was waiting for you to get here today."

"How's it going?" Jake asked. When the foreman came looking for him, generally there was a problem.

"I was wondering if you could go up with me and do a little review of the prints for the next two floors."

"Sure," Jake agreed.

The two men got in the cage that would carry them up to the sixteenth floor, where the foreman's tiny shack sat across a spiderweb of beams.

When they reached the floor, they each snapped onto the safety line that would keep them from falling to their deaths with a single misstep.

"At least the good weather is keeping us on deadline," Brett said as they maneuvered across the beams.

"Before deadline and under budget is always a good thing," Jake replied. "That will make Sam a happy man." Sam Watterson was the owner of the project. Sam was a well-known developer in Kansas City and was involved in dozens of projects.

For the next hour Jake clarified what he needed to with Brett and when he finished he walked around and greeted the workers. He'd always believed being on a first-name basis with the men who were doing the actual work of bringing his blueprints to life was important.

Today it was difficult to make pleasant small talk, but he forced himself to do just that. When he'd finally made the rounds, he returned to his car and sat and watched the work being done.

This building design had been one of several he and Suzanna had worked on together right before her murder. It had been ambitious and bold, and it had taken him the last two years to find the right people to invest in seeing their dream come to life.

It was bittersweet to see it actually being realized without her. There were many nights he and Suzanna would go up and sit on the high beams of one of their construction sites and gaze up at the stars overhead.

Suzanna had always loved the stars and she would point out the various constellations to him. That was why he'd named his business Lamont and Star.

God, he missed her so much. He missed her smiling face. He missed brainstorming with her about new visions of building. He missed talking to her. They had been such an integral part of each other's lives.

An overwhelming grief and a killing guilt pressed down on him. If he'd just made a different decision on that night, then Suzanna would probably be alive today. If he just hadn't been so damned selfish.

He didn't know how long he'd been sitting in the car and thinking of his sister when Monica's car pulled up next to his. He looked at it in surprise. What in the hell was she doing here?

He got out of his car and waited while she exited hers. "Hi." She greeted him with a bright smile. "Did you see the morning paper?"

"I did," he replied.

"We're now famous."

"Not that famous. Our names weren't even mentioned. Is that why you're here?" Clad in white shorts and a bright yellow blouse, she was like a ray of sunshine in what had been a very dark day for him.

"Actually, yes and no," she replied. "I was curious to know if you saw the paper, but I also brought you lunch."

"Lunch?" He stared at her blankly.

"Yeah, you know it's when people eat a meal around noon."

"Did we talk about having lunch together today?" Maybe in the wee hours of the morning while they'd been sitting on Clay's house last night he'd somehow missed something.

"No, we didn't talk about it, but I thought maybe today would be a good day for you to have lunch with your partner."

Her smile and her soft gaze made him realize she knew. She knew it was the anniversary of the day he had found Suzanna's dead body and she had come here to help him get through it.

There was a part of him that wanted to growl at her to go home, to leave him alone with his dark thoughts. She didn't need to be here because she pitied him. That was the last thing he wanted from her.

But then she turned and pulled a picnic basket from her passenger seat and her eyes held a touch of apprehension, as if she knew she might not be welcome. "I hope you like ham and cheese."

And just that quickly he was oddly grateful

she'd shown up. "I love ham and cheese," he replied.

She lit up like a Christmas tree, her eyes sparkling as she smiled widely. "Should we sit in one of the cars?"

"You brought lunch, so I'll provide a dining room." He took the picnic basket from her and then grabbed her hand in his.

He led her around the side of the building where there were several lawn chairs and a couple of sawhorses with sheets of plywood on top. He set the picnic basket in the center of the plywood and then pulled up two chairs.

"It isn't exactly the Ritz," he said.

"But it's perfect for a picnic," she replied, and then opened the picnic basket. The first thing she pulled out was a red-and-white-checkered tablecloth. He helped her put it down, still touched that she was here.

Not only did she have ham-and-cheese sandwiches, but there was also a container of potato salad, small bags of chips, a container of fruit salad and cookies.

"This isn't lunch, this is a feast," he said as she pulled out two cans of soda, then moved the picnic basket to the side.

"I wasn't sure what you normally did for lunch."

"Sometimes I just skip it and other times I grab

a hamburger from a joint down the street," he replied.

The noise of the work site quieted as the men all knocked off for the lunch hour. As he and Monica ate, she asked him questions about the building.

"What's it going to be?" she asked.

"The first floor is going to be a grocery store. They're hoping to draw more people into living in the area and those people will need a place to buy their food."

"And the rest of it?" She looked past his shoulder to the skeletal building.

"The next fifteen floors are office space and the rest of it is going to be lofts for sale."

"I'm not sure I'd want to live in a loft that high up," she replied.

"Are you afraid of heights?" he asked.

"Maybe a little, why?"

"There is no place better to stargaze than on the beams near the top. Suzanna and I used to go up in the high beams and look at the stars. I was just thinking that one night when we aren't doing surveillance, you might be interested in doing a little stargazing with me."

Once again, she looked up at the top of the structure and then gazed back at him. "I imagine it's kind of an exhilarating experience."

"It is."

"There are safety belts or ropes or whatever involved?"

"Definitely."

She looked at him. "Then I'd be up for it."

"We'll do it some night soon." He hadn't been up on the beams at night since Suzanna had died. It was something he hadn't wanted to do by himself when he knew memories of her would assail him.

With Monica it was difficult to be depressed. Something about her filled him with an inexplicable optimism. She reminded him that there was still laughter, and moments of real contentment, real happiness left in the world.

However, none of that really mattered. He could fall madly and wildly in love with her, but he wouldn't act on his feelings.

In any case if she ever learned the role he had played in his sister's murder, she would look at him with revulsion. He'd made a decision that night that he would never forgive himself for and he had a self-loathing that would last for the rest of his life.

"What do you think about dogs?" Her question pulled him back from his dark thoughts.

"I like them better than cats."

"Have you ever thought about getting one?"

"I've thought about it from time to time, but with my work schedule the way it is, it wouldn't be fair to the dog. I'm gone most of the day. Why? Are you thinking about getting one?"

"Maybe. There are times I'd like a little fur baby to keep me company. You know, somebody who thinks I hung the moon and loves me unconditionally." For a moment she looked incredibly vulnerable. Her eyes appeared wistful and then she released a small, uncomfortable laugh and the vulnerability was gone.

"Have you ever had a dog before?" he asked.

"We had a dog when I was young. His name was Pooky and he was the sweetest little schnauzer you'd ever want to meet. He was my cuddle buddy at night and I adored him."

"What happened to him?"

She sighed. "He got heart failure and we had to put him down. I was devastated for a while."

"That's one reason why I don't want a dog. I don't want to bond with a dog that won't live as long as me," he replied.

"But then you miss out on years of laughing and doggy kisses and having a little fur friend that loves you unconditionally. Besides, a dog is a thing to have before babies. It's practice for taking care of something helpless."

He didn't respond to that. He couldn't, because there would never be any babies in his life.

They finished eating and cleaned up and then

he walked her back to her car. He hadn't forgotten why she'd shown up and her thoughtfulness humbled him.

She had pushed away the darkness that had threatened to descend on him. When they reached the car she placed the picnic basket in the seat and then turned back and smiled at him.

"Thank you for taking time out to have lunch with me," she said.

"No, thank you," he replied. She looked so gorgeous, and for just a moment he wanted to pull her up close to him and kiss her smiling, lush lips.

"And now I have a favor to ask you."

"A favor?" He consciously shoved away any thoughts of kissing her.

"I have these two huge steaks and a barbecue grill I don't know how to use. You'd be doing me a big favor if you'd come over this evening and fix them for us."

He looked at her skeptically. "Do you really need me to grill the steaks or are you just being kind?"

"Oh, I definitely need you on the grill." She looked at him innocently. "My father insisted I get one when I bought my house, but the idea of gas and flame scares me a little bit so I've never used it. Besides, you told me you could eat a steak and a baked potato every night, and tonight I'm offering them to you. Besides, I'm really hungry for steak tonight and they just don't taste the same broiled in the oven."

He wanted to tell her no. Things were definitely getting a bit too cozy between them. But when he thought of being at home alone during the long hours of this particular evening with nothing to keep him company but his dark memories, he finally relented.

"Okay. How about six?" He was already going to hell for his role in Suzanna's murder and his part in a pact of death. He might as well add using Monica for company on a difficult night to his sins.

"Perfect," she replied. "I'll text you my address and I'll see you then."

Minutes later he frowned thoughtfully as he watched her drive away from the job site. His desire to have dinner with her tonight was at least partially selfish.

She was like a panacea to his grief, a magic potion that would keep dark memories away. But there was also a bigger part of him that just wanted to spend all his spare time with her, and that's what had him worried.

She was getting under his skin. He found himself thinking about her way too often. Each time he was with her a simmering desire filled his veins.

Her spicy citrus scent enticed him and her easy laughter enchanted him.

He'd go to her house tonight and grill the steaks. He'd enjoy having dinner with her, but after tonight there would be no more meals with her.

They would continue their surveillance, but that would be the extent of the time they spent together.

HE STARED AT the picture in the paper and then slammed his fist onto the faces of Jake Lamont and Monica Wright. Oh yes, he knew who she was. She was a freaking reporter.

Why were the two of them together? Even as he asked himself that question he knew the answer. Jake had turned on them.

How long had the two of them been talking? Why hadn't a news story already appeared detailing the murder pact? Why hadn't any cops come knocking at his door?

He'd known none of the other men would really adhere to their plan of murder. They had all talked a good game that night in the woods, but he knew when push came to shove they wouldn't be able to kill anyone.

He'd taken it upon himself to ensure that four foul pieces of humanity got what they deserved. What he had discovered on that first night when he'd slit Brian McDowell's throat was that he liked it. He'd liked the feel of blood on his hands, the smell of it and the swell of power that filled him as he took the man's life.

He also liked that he had a name…the Vigilante Killer. Only really good killers got names. Hillside Strangler… Son of Sam… Zodiac… Someday the Vigilante Killer would be as well known as those other killers.

He was good at what he did. He'd left no clues, nothing for the police to find him. He had no intention of getting caught or stopping. There were lots of bad people walking around free as birds who needed to be killed.

This was his mission in life. It was his passion and it excited him and he wasn't about to let Jake Lamont run his mouth to a reporter and ruin it all.

He leaned back in his chair and sipped his now-cool coffee. He had no idea why a story hadn't broken yet, but he knew what he had to do. There was no question about it.

They needed to die…sooner rather than later.

Chapter Five

That evening as Jake drove to Monica's house, he couldn't help the way his heart lifted at the anticipation of spending more time with her. And he was still determined that this would be the last time they would spend any social time together. They would continue to do the surveillance together, but that was it.

He sensed that she might be a little bit romantically interested in him, and he wasn't and could never be the kind of man she wanted or deserved. He needed to make sure she understood that he wasn't in the market for any kind of a relationship with her except for a working one. The problem was it was just so damned hard to remember that when she was around him.

He turned down a tree-lined street with small, neat homes and eyed the addresses for hers. Halfway down the block he spied her house. He was interested to see her personal space. He imagined vibrant colors and comfortable furniture.

Her house was a ranch painted a soft gray with darker gray shutters. It sported a maroon front door, and a large picture window in the front reflected the clouds that had moved in late this afternoon.

Pulling up in the driveway, he steeled himself, needing to stay strong and keep his growing feelings for her in check. Maybe she just acted as if she liked him in order to get the story.

He immediately dismissed this idea. She didn't strike him as a woman who would be that disingenuous. He'd already pegged her as a straight shooter and nothing so far had changed that initial assessment of her.

She answered the door on his first knock, and despite all his desires to the contrary, his heart skipped a beat at the sight of her.

Clad in a pair of white shorts and a pink T-shirt that clung to her small waist and emphasized the thrust of her breasts, she looked sexy as hell.

She gestured him into a small but pleasant living room that held a navy blue couch and matching chair and a large flat-screen television anchored on one wall. Bright yellow throw pillows and yellow-based lamps added the vibrant touches he'd imagined would be in her living space. She also had several candles burning and their scents filled the air along with her fragrance.

"The steaks are marinating, baked potatoes are in the oven and a salad is in the fridge," she said as she led him into the kitchen.

It was also a pleasant room, with yellow-and-white curtains hanging at the windows and a bouquet of artificial sunflowers in the center of the round wooden kitchen table.

"How about I check out that grill," he said. Already the scent of her now-familiar perfume eddied in the air as if to torment him.

"It's on the deck." She opened the back door and together they went out on the deck, where a table with a bright blue umbrella was already set with navy-and-yellow-ringed dinner plates.

"Since the clouds moved in and it's not as hot as it has been, I thought we'd eat out here if that's all right with you."

"Perfect," he replied. At least out here he wouldn't have her scent surrounding him.

The grill was a standard gas one and it took him only minutes to get it lit and warming up. "How does a cold beer sound?" she asked.

"It sounds great."

"I'll be right back." She disappeared into the kitchen.

He walked over to the deck railing and gazed

out to her backyard. There were several pretty trees and a birdbath in a round flower bed. The grass was neatly cut and the whole thing was surrounded by a privacy fence.

He turned as she came back outside. "Thanks." He took the icy beer bottle from her. He twisted off the top and took a drink. "Ah, there's nothing better than a cold beer on a warm day."

"I completely agree." She took a sip of her beer and then set it down on the table. "Just let me know when you're ready for the steaks."

"We'll let the grill warm up for a few more minutes. I was just admiring your backyard. With the fence it would be perfect for that little fur baby you mentioned."

She smiled. "I know. I'm trying to decide if I'm ready to make that kind of commitment."

"Do you know what kind of dog you'd like?"

"I've been thinking about it and I'm leaning toward a miniature schnauzer, since that's what I had growing up and a girlfriend of mine has one now and he's a little sweetheart."

"Sounds like a good choice," he replied. "You have a very nice home."

She laughed. "Thanks, but it's nothing but a mud hut compared to yours."

"That's not true," he said with a laugh of his own. "Besides, I had to build a house that reflected my profession. It's a big house for just one person to ramble around in and it's easy to be lonely there." Embarrassment filled him and he mentally kicked himself. Even though it was true, why had he said that out loud?

She looked at him for a long moment. "I get lonely, too. I guess it doesn't matter how big or small your house is. People can be lonely anywhere."

He broke eye contact with her. "Maybe we both need dogs." He walked over to the grill. "I think it's ready for the steaks."

She brought him two beautiful T-bones and as they sizzled on the grill they talked about the weather and the clouds that had moved in. They argued about what made a perfect steak—he believed it should be medium-rare and she insisted well-done was better.

What they didn't talk about was loneliness or anything else personal. The easy conversation continued as they ate. They shared more about their work and then talked about sports. They both loved football and supported the local Chiefs team.

"There's nothing better than tailgating at a Kansas City Chiefs game."

"I know, all you can smell is good barbecue," he replied.

"When you're at home and watching a football game what kind of food do you eat?" she asked.

"Hot wings and french fries."

"Ah, a man after my own heart." Her eyes sparkled brightly. "I love hot wings dipped in blue cheese dressing."

"No way," he replied. "They're better if they're dipped in ranch dressing."

Then followed a discussion about the best foods to eat while watching a football game.

He pushed his empty plate away. "That was one delicious steak, and the potato was baked to perfection."

"I hope you have enough room for dessert," she said. "I bought a peach pie."

"For peach pie, I might have a little room left."

When she was finished eating night had fallen, and they cleared their dishes and moved inside where she made coffee and then cut them each a piece of the pie.

They settled on the sofa side by side to eat the dessert and once again her scent surrounded him. She placed her hand on his arm. He'd come to realize that she was naturally a toucher. He was sure she had no idea how her frequent touches warmed him.

"Tell me about your sister, Jake," she said. "Tell me what Suzanna was like."

He stared at her and for a moment his heart stopped beating. What was she doing? Why did she want to talk about his sister? He hadn't talked to anyone about Suzanna in the past two years. He wasn't even sure he could. He placed his empty pie dish on the coffee table and then looked at Monica once again.

Her gaze was soft, inviting him to share. "Why do you want to know about her?" He heard the thick emotion in his voice and coughed in an effort to clear it.

"I want to know all about her because she was so important to you."

He closed his eyes for a moment, wondering if he could do this. Could he reach beyond the darkness to find the light that had been his sister? "She had the most incredible laugh," he finally said, and opened his eyes.

Speaking that simple sentence seemed to loosen not only the lump in his throat, but also a dam inside him. "It was one of those kinds of laughs that invited everyone around her to share in it even if they didn't know what they were laughing about."

"That's a wonderful gift." She scooted closer to him on the sofa. "Tell me more, Jake. Isn't today a good day for celebrating her life instead of dwelling on her death?"

Celebrating her life? He'd never thought about

it before, but that's exactly what he wanted to do right now with Monica. "I liked to tease her about being a pesky little sister. She was almost two minutes younger than me and I never let her forget that I was the older, wiser one."

He leaned back, suddenly immersed in good memories. "She was so full of life. She loved roller coasters and scary movies, but she also loved growing flowers and stargazing and listening to classical music."

He took a sip of his coffee and then continued, "She used to tell me I had the social graces of an ox. But she drew people to her. She had lots of friends and she was loyal and supportive of all of them. Have you ever seen a picture of her?"

Monica shook her head. "No, I haven't."

He pulled his wallet from his back pocket and with fingers that trembled slightly, he pulled out the picture he carried of the sister he'd lost. He handed the small photo to Monica.

She studied the picture for several moments and then handed it back to him. "She was beautiful."

"She wasn't just beautiful on the outside, she was also beautiful on the inside." He tucked the picture away and returned his wallet to his back pocket.

"I had to start scaring guys away from her when we were only about thirteen." He smiled. "I have to admit there were a couple of years where she hated me for playing the role of big bad father."

Monica laughed. "So you scared all the boys?"

"I did. I finally eased up a bit when she was about seventeen. She dated a lot but managed to keep up her grades. And she always seemed to date nice boys, which also helped me relax."

"You mentioned that your parents were both drug addicts and died when the two of you were young. How on earth did you two manage to survive?"

"Needless to say, we both had to grow up really fast. There were many nights we were the caretakers for them rather than the other way around. We hoarded any change or dollar bills we'd find and use that to buy food. We quickly learned what food went the furthest, but of course there were days when there was no food to be found. I'm not telling you this so you will feel sorry for me, but rather to show you that it was always Suzanna and me against the world."

"How did you manage to put yourselves through college?"

"We figured out early on that education was the only way we were going to get out of the life we were living and make something of ourselves. We both got scholarships and grants, and then when we turned twenty-one we were shocked to learn that our mother's father left us an inheritance that helped us. We both worked and then used the inheritance to pay off college debt. We used what was left over to open our business."

"Your mother's parents…they didn't step in to help you and Suzanna?"

"My mother's mother died when she was fairly young so it was just our grandfather, who we'd only met once. He died when we were young, and I don't think my parents even knew about an inheritance. A lawyer contacted us on our twenty-first birthday, which was the term set up in his will."

"And you and Suzanna worked well together?"

"We did. It was nice for me to have a partner who could finish my sentences and who saw the world like me. Yet her weaknesses were my strengths and vice versa. She was good at visualizing the amazing buildings, and my strength was the actual drawing up the blueprints of her vision."

"You hear horror stories about family going into business together," Monica replied.

He nodded. "We talked about that and both of us agreed our relationship came first and was far more important than the business. Everything worked beautifully until she started dating Max Clinton."

He frowned and his jaw clenched tight as he remembered the first time Suzanna had introduced him to Max Clinton. Even then there had been several little red flags that had waved in his head, but he'd kept his concerns to himself.

At that first meeting Max had shown hints of being a control freak and gave the impression that Suzanna was a piece of property he'd just newly acquired. Then he'd told himself he had misunderstood and was just imagining things.

"She was absolutely crazy about him. He was a good-looking guy and smooth as silk." He got up from the sofa and walked over to the picture window. He stared out even though he couldn't see anything except the darkness of the night.

"Within three months of them dating she'd moved him into her house. I started getting worried when I realized not only was he slowly isolating her from all her friends and me, but he also had a huge jealous streak."

"Definitely two big red flags."

He turned back around to face Monica. "Yeah, and it got worse from there. She started showing up at the office with cuts and bruises. She even had a couple of black eyes during that time. But she always had some kind of crazy explanation for the injuries."

He drew in a deep breath and released it slowly. "She finally confessed to me that he had a temper and she was tired of being his punching bag.

She threw him out of her house, and I hoped and prayed that was the end of it."

"But it wasn't," Monica said softly.

"No, it wasn't." His chest tightened with a twist of turbulent emotions and once again he clenched his jaw at the memories that now raced to the forefront of his mind.

"She became a cliché for an abused woman. He'd send her flowers and sweet-talk her and she'd welcome him back. I now know that's called the honeymoon period in an abusive relationship. Then he'd beat her again and she'd throw him out. It was a vicious cycle that I couldn't break. I tried to talk to her, I yelled at her, but ultimately all I could do was just sit back and watch it all happen."

He was vaguely aware of Monica getting up from the sofa and joining him in front of the window. But he was deep now into memories that weren't a celebration of his sister's life, but rather the utter tragedy of her untimely death.

"He was in and out of her house a dozen times, and each time when she threw him out, he got more and more angry. The last time she seemed determined to make a final break with him. First, he pleaded and cajoled her to take him back, and when she refused, he stalked her and he left messages that he was going to kill her...the 'if I can't have you, nobody will' kinds of threats."

Jake's emotions threatened to spiral out of control. His chest was so tight he could hardly draw a breath. The back of his throat had closed up as pain and regret pummeled him.

Monica placed her hand on his shoulder and moved closer to him. He couldn't talk about this anymore. They both knew how it had ended. Only he knew his part in it all and he would never voice his own culpability aloud to anyone. That was a shame, a guilt that was too enormous for words.

He stared at Monica helplessly, unable to speak and caught in emotions too deep to share. She returned his gaze and moved closer to him. She raised her face. "Kiss me, Jake."

Her words shocked him, and that shock cast his memories aside. He gazed down at her and became aware of the heat of her body so tight against his and how soft and welcoming her slightly parted lips appeared.

Even though he knew it was wrong on so many levels, he lowered his head and captured her lips with his. All thoughts of Suzanna slipped out of his mind as Monica raised her arms to curl around his neck and opened her mouth to deepen their kiss.

He hadn't realized how cold he'd been until the fire in her kiss, the intimate press of her body against his, warmed him. And he welcomed the warmth by deepening the kiss and tangling his fingers in the long, silky strands of her hair.

She welcomed him. Her tongue swirled with his as her arms tightened around his neck. He was quickly lost in her; any other thoughts were impossible.

Suddenly, the picture window exploded as rapid gunshots filled the air.

MONICA SCREAMED AS Jake threw her down to the floor and then covered her body with his. Bullets whizzed into the wall opposite the window, shattering the glass on the pictures that had hung there. They slammed into the Sheetrock, chipping out chunks with their impact.

Terror shot through her, making it difficult for her to draw a breath. And yet she had to be breathing because in some place in the back of her mind she knew she was screaming and sobbing.

The noise was deafening, and she clung to Jake, squeezing her fingers into his shoulders as she continued to sob. What was happening? Why was this happening? Her brain couldn't wrap around it. Who was shooting into her house?

It seemed to go on forever. Finally, it stopped. There was the squeal of tires on pavement. And then silence. Except for the deep sobs that Monica couldn't seem to control.

"It's okay. We're okay," Jake whispered in her ear. She knew he meant to comfort her, but his voice was deep with tension. "Monica, we're fine."

Fine? No, she wasn't fine. Somebody had just tried to kill her and terror still squeezed her throat half-closed, still iced her entire body.

"I'm going to get up and I want you to crawl down the hallway and into the bathroom," he said.

The bathroom? At the moment it felt like it was a million miles away from the living room. Still, it was an interior place in the house. He was sending her to an interior room.

"Do…do you think they'll be back?" Oh God, this was a nightmare, the worst nightmare she'd ever suffered. And she couldn't wake up.

"I don't think they'll be back, but just to be on the safe side, I want you in the bathroom until the police arrive. Now, are you ready?"

No, no, she wasn't ready. She didn't want him to get up from her. She needed his body next to hers, making her feel safe despite the horrifying event that had just occurred.

"Monica?"

"Yes, okay," she replied. Her sobs had subsided for the moment, but her heart still beat so quickly she felt dizzy and breathless.

Jake rose from her but remained in a low crouch as she crawled toward the hallway. She tried to avoid moving through the broken glass that littered the floor, and by the time she reached the bathroom she was crying once again.

She closed the door and sat with her back against the tub. Her tears half-choked her and her ears still rang with the sound of the bullets flying.

Somebody had just tried to kill her…them. Who had done this? Who was responsible? Never had she felt such terror.

What was Jake doing out there? Surely he had called the police by now. And even if he hadn't she would imagine one of her neighbors had called. Gunshots in this neighborhood never happened.

There had been so many bullets. She didn't know much about guns, but if there had only been one person shooting then they had to have used some sort of a semiautomatic weapon.

Who had done this? The question pounded in her head like a bad headache. And would they come back again? Was it possible this had to do with the gang podcasts she'd been doing?

Nothing in her life had prepared her for something like this happening. Even when she'd pressed to be Jake's partner in finding the Vigilante Killer, she hadn't believed she'd be in any real danger.

Tonight had been real and present danger.

She drew in several deep breaths in an effort to

stanch her tears. Who did this? The question re-peated again and again in her head.

The sound of sirens caused a shuddery relief to flood her. She swallowed the last of her sobs and then quickly swiped at her cheeks.

Surely the shooter wouldn't come back with the police here. She got to her feet and opened the bathroom door. The sound of Jake's voice along with several others assured her that it was okay to leave the bathroom.

She walked on unsteady legs into the living room, where Jake was speaking to three police officers. Jake gestured her to his side and, on legs that still shook, she joined them.

Jake introduced her to Officers Tim Moran, Brad McDonald and Stephanie Boen. "So, what do you think happened here tonight?" Officer Boen asked her.

"I don't know what happened," Monica replied. "We were just talking and all of a sudden the win-dow exploded and bullets were flying." Her voice trembled, and she was grateful when Jake threw an arm around her shoulder and pulled her closer to his side. "We could have been killed. We should be dead right now." She stopped talking and drew in another deep breath as she heard her own hys-terical voice.

"I've caught your podcast several times, Ms.

Wright," Officer McDonald said. "Is it possible one of your stories is the cause of what happened here tonight?"

Monica told them about the gang series she was running, and then Jake reminded her about Larry Albright. She told the officers about the threatening messages he'd left her and about him following her to the restaurant and throwing a beer bottle at her.

"It's a big leap from throwing a bottle at me and what happened tonight," she said. Looking around the room her chill returned, and she began to shiver once again. "Whoever did this wanted to kill me." A new hollow wind of fear blew through her.

Jake tightened his arm around her. "We aren't going to let that happen."

For the next hour or so they were questioned over and over again while other officials dug bullets out of her walls. When that evidence had been collected, all them left except Officer McDonald.

"I'll be honest with you, this has all the markings of a typical gang-related drive-by shooting," he told them, and then looked at Monica. "Do you have some place you can stay for the rest of the night?"

"She does," Jake answered for her.

"In fact, I would recommend you stay away

from here even longer than a night," the officer continued. "If you have ticked off somebody in the gang world, then you probably need to see if a little time will cool things off and maybe talk to the men who were on your podcast."

This couldn't be her life. It couldn't be true that somebody wanted her dead. And yet it was true, and she'd never been so frightened.

She listened absently as Officer McDonald said they would investigate the crime. But he also said that drive-by shootings were particularly difficult to solve. "I'll sit out at the curb until you two leave here." And then he was gone.

Monica became aware of the hot air wafting in where the front window used to be. Somewhere in the neighborhood several dogs barked. It was all so surreal. Her house now felt like an alien space and not the sanctuary she'd always believed it to be.

"Do you have anything we can use to cover the window until we can get it fixed?" Jake asked.

"Uh… I think there might be some plywood out in my shed," she replied. Her voice sounded weak and trembling even to her own ears. "There's also a hammer and nails in there."

"Why don't you come into the kitchen and sit while I see about finding material to board up the window."

"Okay." She was suddenly eager to get out of the living room, where despite the officer's car being parked, another round of bullets could come in unimpeded by a glass window. Would the shooter or shooters come back?

In the kitchen she handed him the shed key and then she sank down in a chair at the table. "Jake... be careful. They might come back." Sadly, even policemen could be killed in a hail of bullets. She bit back tears that threatened to fall again.

"I don't think they'll be back," he replied. "For all they know right now, we're both dead. Sit tight and I'll get this taken care of in no time." He disappeared out the back door.

For all they know right now, we're both dead. His words played and replayed in her mind. She chewed on her index fingernail as a million other thoughts flew through her head.

If the shooting was gang-related, then she didn't know why. Her interviews with the gang members had not focused on their criminal activities, but rather on what had drawn them to that lifestyle and what they believed needed to be done to solve the gang issues in the city. The men she had talked to had been more than cooperative. They had appeared pleased that somebody was actually listening to them. So why would they come after her now?

And if she needed to stay away from here for a few days, where would she go? Her father lived in a small house and he didn't even have a bed in either of the guest rooms. One held workout equipment and the other room he used as a storage area. She would die if she had to go to one of her sister's homes. She didn't want to hear them tsk-tsking her over her lifestyle or career.

She'd go to a motel even though the idea of being all alone was abhorrent right now. Tears once again pressed hot behind her eyes.

What was taking Jake so long? Had somebody been hiding in her shed? Or in the darkness of her backyard? Had he been attacked? She stared at the back door, her heartbeat accelerating with a new fear.

What if Jake had been jumped? Maybe he was right now in the backyard unconscious or...

Just when she thought she might scream, he came back in. He carried a hammer and half a sheet of plywood. He leaned the plywood against the wall. "This should do it," he said. "But I'm going to need your help."

She jumped out of the chair. "Let's do it." Anything to take her mind off her horrible thoughts.

It took them only fifteen minutes to position the wood over the opening the missing glass had created and nail it solidly in place.

"Now pack some bags. You're going to stay with me," he said.

"Really? I'm supposed to stay away from here for more than a night." She stared at him, wanting nothing more than his arms around her.

He seemed to sense her need, for he pulled her into his arms. "You'll be safe at my place for as long as you need to be there," he whispered into her ear. "I have lights and alarms and mean guard dogs with sharp teeth who will go after anyone who gets close to my house."

A small laugh released from her. He held her only a moment longer and then let go of her. "Now go pack up what you'll need to be away from here for a week or so. While you're doing that, I'll do a little cleanup in the living room. Broom?"

"In the pantry," she replied.

As he began to sweep the hardwood floor, she went into her office. The first thing she packed was her work equipment. She'd wanted a story and now she had one, but she wished she didn't. Tonight real danger had come far too close. If it wasn't for Jake's quick action in pulling her to the floor, they both would have been dead, their bodies riddled with bullets.

With her equipment all packed up, she went

from her office into her bedroom and pulled out a large suitcase from her closet. She had moved from paralyzing fear to a curious numbness.

The numbness kept its grip on her as she packed clothes and toiletries. She then went back into the living room, where Jake was sweeping up the last of the broken glass from the floor.

Even without the broken glass, the room looked like a war zone. The wall was riddled with holes and all the pictures she'd had hanging were ruined. Even though she knew it wasn't true and it was just her imagination, right now the room smelled evil.

Would she ever feel safe here again? She didn't know the answer. All she knew for sure was she was ready to go anyplace but here.

"Let's get your things loaded into my car and get out of here," Jake said, as if he'd read her thoughts.

She didn't breathe easier until they were in his car and driving down the street away from her house.

"Are you okay?" he asked softly.

"I'm not sure," she admitted. "Right now I just feel kind of numb."

"Maybe numb is good for right now."

"At least I'm not screaming or sobbing. I'm

sorry you had to put up with that. There's nothing worse than having to deal with a hysterical woman."

He flashed her a quick glance. "Don't be silly. Trust me, I was definitely screaming on the inside."

She studied his profile, illuminated by the dashboard lights. "Are you sure you want me at your house?"

He smiled reassuringly at her. "Monica, I have a big house with two guest rooms. I want to make sure you're safe, so yes, I want you at my house. I just hope you're not an irritatingly cheerful morning person."

To her surprise she laughed. "Trust me, I'm not anything near a cheerful morning person. Truthfully, I'm pretty grouchy when I first wake up." She sobered and continued to gaze at him. His handsome features looked strong and she found comfort in the strength that emanated from him.

Suddenly she was thinking about what had happened just before the bullets had flown. The kiss. Oh, that amazing kiss. It had torched a wonderful heat that had sizzled through her from the top of her head to the very tips of her toes.

His mouth had been demanding and hungry against hers and she wondered what else might have happened between them if the window hadn't been shot out.

Now she was going to be staying in his house and despite everything that had happened, right now all she could think about was if and when he might kiss her again.

Chapter Six

Jake sat at his kitchen table with his hands wrapped around a cup of coffee. Dawn's light drifted in the window, bringing with it the promise of a new day.

He was exhausted. He'd barely slept the night before. He'd gotten Monica settled into one of his guest rooms and she had immediately gone to bed.

He'd been too pumped up with adrenaline to sleep and had sat in his recliner for hours with his brain working overtime. Many of those same thoughts still whirled around in his head right now.

Death had come far too close to them the night before. If they hadn't hit the floor quickly enough they both would have been killed.

His inclination was to believe it had been a result of Monica's podcast. It was the only answer that really made sense. Still, he'd considered that it was possible it was the Vigilante Killer who had somehow gotten word that he was talking to a reporter. He supposed it was possible the murderer had seen their picture in the paper. But the attack wasn't the style of that particular killer and so he'd dismissed that idea.

Even though the odds were against them, he hoped like hell the police could figure out who was behind the assault and get him, her or them behind bars.

He took a sip of his coffee and thought about the woman who was now asleep beneath navy sheets in his guest room. She had caught him by surprise last night. *Kiss me, Jake.* When she'd said that to him he hadn't been able to do anything else but comply.

Kissing her had been breathtaking. The softness of her lips…the warmth of her body against his, had dizzied his senses with desire. She had immediately banished the grief that had welled up inside him when he'd been talking about Suzanna.

If the bullets hadn't flown, what else might have happened between them? If she'd said, "Make love to me, Jake," would they have wound up in her bedroom? Or would he have come to his senses and stopped that from happening? He honestly didn't know the answer to that question.

His feelings for her were crazy and all wrong. The last thing he wanted was to lead her on, to make her believe he was interested in a long-term relationship with her.

Despite the fact that she was now under his roof, he had to keep his distance from her. There was no question she was a temptation, but kissing her had been wrong and he couldn't let anything like that happen between them again.

Once they identified the Vigilante Killer, the odds were good he'd never see her again. She'd have her big story and he'd go back to the life he deserved…forever alone and without love or laughter in his life.

He was still seated at the table sipping coffee and thumbing through the morning paper at just after nine o'clock when Monica appeared. Clad in a navy blue robe and with her hair sleep-tousled, she looked utterly charming…except for the frown that rode her features.

"Coffee is in the pot," he said. "Cups are in the cabinet above the coffeepot."

She nodded and beelined in that direction. He watched as she grabbed a cup, filled it, and then walked to the table and sat in a chair opposite him.

She didn't speak and neither did he. She also didn't look at him. She took a drink of her coffee and then stared into the cup as if it might hold the answers to all the age-old questions.

He'd been warned that she was crabby when she first woke up and she definitely looked crabby. There was nothing about her that invited any conversation. When she'd finished off one cup of coffee, she went back to the countertop and refilled her cup. When she returned to the table she took a couple of sips, leaned back in her chair and released a deep sigh.

She looked at him with a sheepish grin. "Thank you for respecting my morning crankiness by not trying to talk to me."

"The frown on your face was enough to scare anyone mute," he teased.

She winced. "Was it that bad?"

He nodded. "It was that bad."

"I don't know why I wake up in such a bad mood. I've been that way since I was a little girl and of course both my sisters and my dad are bright-eyed, cheerful morning people. I remember wanting to smash them all in their happy faces with a waffle."

He laughed and then sobered. "How did you sleep?"

"I was afraid I would have nightmares all night long, but I went out like a light and didn't suffer from any bad dreams."

"That's good."

"What about you?"

"I had a restless night," he admitted. "I didn't have any bad dreams but I just couldn't shut off my brain enough to fall asleep."

"I hate nights like that. I'm sorry, Jake. I'm sorry about all of this."

"Did you hire somebody to shoot up your house?" he asked gently.

Her eyes widened. "Of course not."

"Monica, you have nothing to apologize for."

She offered him a small smile. "Thanks, I guess I needed to hear that." She leaned forward and he caught a whiff of her scent. "I was wondering if there's someplace in your house I could set up my equipment so I can continue to do my podcasts in the evenings."

Of course her first thought would be about her work. She was ambitious. And he was an arrogant fool to think that her asking him to kiss her the night before had anything to do with her wanting a relationship with him.

He'd been emotional about Suzanna's death at the time she'd asked him to kiss her. It had probably been done in an effort to comfort him and had meant nothing to her.

"We can set you up in my office. I'm not doing any work in there right now. It has a big drafting table that can be folded down to give you plenty of space for all your equipment."

"That sounds awesome." She gave him a bright smile. Even with a bit of raccoon eyes and no other makeup, she looked beautiful.

He got up from the table. "Are you up for some breakfast?"

"Thanks, but I'm not really much of a break-fast eater." She lifted her cup. "I prefer to drink my breakfast."

"Yeah, I'm not much of a morning eater, either." He leaned his back against the counter. The smell of her had stirred him and he found himself won-dering what she had on beneath the short blue robe.

Get a grip, Lamont, he told himself firmly. If he couldn't keep those kinds of thoughts out of his head then it was going to be one hell of a long week.

She finished her second cup of coffee and then rose. "I think I'll go jump in the shower and get dressed for the day. Then if you could show me your office, I'd appreciate it."

"I'm ready whenever you are," he replied.

He breathed a sigh of relief when she left the kitchen. He had a feeling having her here was going to be more difficult than he'd initially thought.

He had to keep a tight control of his emotions where she was concerned. She was just a house-guest who needed a place to stay, not a potential lover he was wooing.

He rinsed their cups and placed them in the dishwasher and then stepped outside on his back deck. The clouds from the night before had brought no rain and it looked to be another dry, hot day. No rain was fine with him; it kept the construction on the job site going.

Thank God there had been no report of another Vigilante murder in the morning paper. Going to sit on Clay's house had been the last thing on his mind the night before. All he'd wanted to do was get Monica out of her house and here where he could assure her safety.

When he'd driven her here from her house he'd made sure they weren't followed. If the shooting was gang-related, there was no way anyone from that world would think to look for her here.

He wouldn't be surprised if she wanted to put the whole Vigilante hunting on hold. If that was the case, then she could stay here, and he would continue to sit on Clay's place during the killing hours.

Although he had joked about having alarms and killer dogs to guard the house, what he did have was a state-of-the-art alarm system and strong locks on each of his doors and windows. He was confident she would be safe here.

Thirty minutes later she returned to the kitchen. Wearing a pair of denim shorts and a red-and-white-striped tank top, she looked fresh and ready to officially face the day.

"All ready for me to set you up in the office?" he asked.

"I just need to grab my equipment from my bedroom."

"I'll help you with that." He knew her bags were heavy from carrying them into the house the night before.

He followed her down the hallway to the room he'd given her to stay in. It was a nice room, big and airy and with its own bathroom.

She'd made the bed up with the navy-and-light-blue spread and matching throw pillows. The room smelled of her scent, that wonderful, slightly exotic fragrance that made his pulse race just a little bit faster.

It would have been so much easier if he hadn't kissed her. If he didn't have the memory of her soft lips beneath his, then he wouldn't be thinking about kissing her again right now.

Minutes later they were in his home office, where they unloaded her equipment and she set it up on the desk. Behind the desk was a historic picture of downtown Kansas City, which she proclaimed would make a wonderful backdrop for her podcast.

"This is great, thank you so much," she said when they were finished. "What are your plans for the rest of the day?"

"I'm leaving here pretty quick to check in at the job site and I thought you might want to come take the ride with me."

"Oh, I was hoping I'd be here all alone so I could sneak a peek in your underwear drawer and then go through your closet." She paused a beat, as if waiting for his outraged response.

He smiled at her. "I'm afraid you'll be bored to death by both. I prefer boxers over briefs and there are no skeletons rattling around in my closet."

She laughed. "Ah, you're quick, Mr. Lamont. I'm happy to go with you as long as I have enough time later this afternoon to do some research and work on this evening's podcast." Any laughter that had been in her eyes disappeared. "I have to tell you, it's really hard for me to believe that last night's shooting was in any way tied to my podcasts about the gang issue."

He frowned. "Then what do you think it was about?"

Her eyes darkened. "I think it's possible it was the Vigilante Killer." Her voice was a whisper, as if she was afraid the killer might hear her talking about him.

Jake frowned. "I wondered about that earlier, but what happened last night really isn't his style."

"Forget his style. I'm wondering if he saw our picture in the paper and freaked out. He was watching my house and when he saw the two of us together in the window. We made perfect targets and he tried to kill us both."

She stared at him, as if willing him to protest that particular scenario. But he couldn't. He didn't know who had been behind the attack the night before and he didn't know what was worse: a gang that wanted Monica silenced or a killer who feared identification, knew where he lived and now wanted both Monica and him dead.

MONICA HAD TO ADMIT, she wasn't over last night's attack. She'd never considered that her choice of career would put her in any danger. Sure, she'd known on some intellectual level that when she partnered up with Jake to find the killer there was a possibility of danger. However, thinking about it intellectually and actually experiencing it were two very different things.

Jake told her she could stay at the house while he checked in at his job site. He'd even shown her the alarm system and how to set it, but the truth of the matter was she wasn't ready to be left alone.

Before they left the house he went into his bedroom and came out wearing his jeans and a lightweight navy blazer over a white T-shirt. "You're looking pretty spiffy to go to the job site," she observed.

"Get used to the blazer," he replied, and opened one side to reveal a shoulder holster with a gun. "I have a concealed carry license and I intend to carry anytime we leave the house."

It was a sobering moment and yet she had to admit she felt safer knowing he was armed.

As they drove to his job site she found herself looking over her shoulder to the cars behind them, needing to make sure they weren't being followed by anyone.

"Try to relax," Jake said. "Whoever might be after us, they're like cockroaches that only come out at night."

"Do you really believe that?" she asked anxiously.

"I do. If it's gang-related, those kinds of things usually happen after dark. If it was the Vigilante Killer, I know those men we suspect have day jobs, and it would be important for them to show up there every day so when an investigation happens nobody thinks there's anything odd going on with them."

She settled back in her seat and tried to relax, but her heartbeat remained slightly accelerated and her nerves were on edge.

"While you're out talking to the men on the site, I'm going to make some phone calls. I'm going to try to make contact with some of the gang members who are part of the podcast series. Maybe one of them can tell us what's going on."

"Sounds like a good plan," he replied.

It wasn't until they reached Jake's job site that she began to relax. She remained in the car as Jake checked in with the men who were working.

He was greeted with wide smiles and obvious respect from each of the men he spoke to. She wasn't surprised. Jake was a stand-up, regular kind of guy and Monica found those traits very appealing.

In fact she was finding everything about Jake appealing. His body was hot and his laughter was as infectious as he'd described his sister's. He was smart and he made her feel safe and he...

She consciously willed her thoughts away from the man who was supposed to be her business partner of sorts and instead focused on what she wanted to run on her podcast that night.

She definitely intended to report the shooting that had occurred at her house and she had another gang member interview to run. She also had to take some time to research what else was big, local news that her audience would be interested in.

She only had a phone number for two of the men who had agreed to be a part of the gang series. She dialed the first number and a robot voice declared that it was not a working number. The second call she made went to an answering machine. She left a message but she doubted she'd hear anything back.

As she thought of her podcast for the night, she realized she'd better call her father to let him know she was okay. If her family watched, they'd know she was all right, but she seriously doubted any of them had ever watched her show. If they heard about the shooting from any other source, they might freak out. Of course, nobody had called her so she doubted they even knew what was going on in her life.

Maybe she just needed to hear the sound of her father's deep voice. She dialed him and he answered on the second ring. "What's up?" he asked.

She explained to him about the shooting and before she was completely finished he was already cursing. "If you had a real damn job, crap like this wouldn't happen."

Instantly, hot tears burned at her eyes. "Dad, I just called to let you know I'm safe and staying with a friend."

"A friend? Last I heard you didn't have any friends because you always have your nose in the internet. So, who is this friend?"

"His name is Jake and I'm going to be staying in his house for the next week or so."

"Is this guy a boyfriend?" There was a touch of hope in his voice.

"No, we're just friends," she replied quickly.

"Hmm, too bad. It's past time for you to find a good man and get married. You know you aren't getting any younger. I don't want you to wake up one day and be one of those old ladies living with a bunch of cats."

She laughed. "Dad, you know I'm not fond of cats and I just turned thirty. I have plenty of time to get married and have babies."

"Maybe you could give me a grandson. All your sisters have managed to spit out are more girls."

"And you're crazy about those girls," she replied. Her father might be gruff and outspoken, but he was a marshmallow when he was around his granddaughters.

"But if you don't get off this podcast nonsense you're never going to have a normal life."

She sighed. "I'll call you tomorrow, okay?" She was grateful to end the call. The conversation had been depressing. Most of her conversations with her father were depressing.

Why couldn't he be proud of her, of what she did and who she was as a person? Why did she always get the feeling that she was never quite enough for him?

Fifteen minutes later Jake returned to the car. "I thought we'd drive through and get some Chinese to take home and warm up for dinner tonight."

"Sounds good to me." *Is this guy a boyfriend?* Her father's question whispered through her head. As they pulled away from the job site, she shot surreptitious glances at the man behind the wheel.

She wouldn't mind if he was her boyfriend. She wouldn't mind at all if they ate Chinese for dinner and then they went into his master bedroom and got into bed together. As her boyfriend, he would hold her and make sweet love to her and then she'd fall asleep in his arms. That scenario sounded far too appealing at the moment.

Casting her gaze out the passenger window, she chided herself. She couldn't get all crazy about Jake. It wasn't time for her to find her one true love. She needed to prove herself a success in her work before she could even think about falling in love.

"You're awfully quiet," Jake said, breaking into her thoughts. "Are you okay?"

"I'm fine. I just had a conversation with my father and he usually manages to depress me a little," she confessed.

"I'm sorry," he replied. He reached over and placed his hand over hers on the console. The physical touch lasted only a moment and then he returned his hand to the steering wheel.

But the warmth of that simple touch remained with her.

She had to get her head on straight. Jake had to remain a means to an end and nothing more. "I hope you're planning on us sitting on Clay's house again tonight."

"Given what happened last night, I wasn't sure where your thoughts might be about resuming that," he replied.

"I'm still all in," she replied firmly. "The sooner something breaks in that case, the sooner I'll be out of your life."

He cast her a glance. "I'm in no real hurry for you to be out of my life." Butterflies flew in the pit of her stomach. "I want to make sure you're completely safe before that happens."

The butterflies halted their flight and disappeared. He wanted her safe. He didn't want her in his life any longer than necessary. He just wanted her…safe. Once again, she stared out the passenger window and wondered why his words somehow depressed her all over again.

HE'D MISSED. THEY hadn't died. Although he would have preferred to slit their throats like he had so many before them, his main goal had been to kill them as quickly and as efficiently as possible.

When he'd seen them standing in the window at Monica's house he'd made his move, firing as many bullets as possible before driving away.

He'd been so sure he'd killed them, but the morning news had only had a short report of the shooting, indicating that nobody had been hurt.

Damn. Damn! How had they survived that hail of bullets? Besides needing to take care of them as soon as possible, he was also hungering for the feel of blood on his hands again.

The morning news had also included a story about a man who was arrested for killing a dog and he had been released to await his trial. He hadn't been arrested for the death of the dog, but rather for carrying a handgun without a license.

The man, Greg Bellows, insisted the dog had attacked him and he'd had to kill the animal to save his own life. He'd been carrying a friend's gun that morning on his walk because the dog had attacked him before.

He didn't believe Greg's story and anyone who could hurt an innocent animal was scum of the earth.

And he was the self-anointed destroyer of scum. Greg would never make it before a judge. He had already judged him guilty, and his sentence was death.

His fingers tingled and his heart raced as he thought of the look of surprise Greg would have on his face right before his throat was slit.

Tonight the Vigilante Killer would take care of

Greg. After that his next kills had to be Jake and Monica. They had to die before Jake talked too much and Monica broke a story that might lead the cops to him.

It was important that the Vigilante Killer survive and thrive. There were just so many people who needed to die.

Chapter Seven

Dammit. The killer had struck again. Jake read the article in the morning paper and a wave of anger and renewed guilt swept through him.

He didn't know the victim, but what scared him was Greg Bellows had been charged, but not yet tried for his offense. He should have been presumed innocent, but the Vigilante Killer had not only tried him and found him guilty, he'd also handed out the ultimate punishment…death.

This had been Jake's biggest fear. The killer was escalating, no longer murdering the last of the men's perpetrators connected to the pact, but apparently going after anyone he deemed guilty. The thought was absolutely horrifying.

Last night they had continued their surveillance on Clay's house and now Jake knew with certainty Clay wasn't the killer. That left Adam. Jake felt the pressing need to get him arrested, but he had no real evidence to offer the authorities.

He needed to catch Adam in the act. Unfortunately, it would probably be a week or so before the killer acted again. Just the thought of the man going after somebody created a knot of tension in the pit of his stomach. He hoped like hell the killer made a mistake with this latest murder. He hoped the police found something that would lead them to making an arrest.

He looked up from the paper as Monica stumbled into the kitchen. She got a cup of coffee, sat across from him and offered him a half smile.

He raised an eyebrow. "This can't be cranky Monica actually smiling before a couple of cups of coffee."

"I'm trying to change my ways." She took a sip of her drink and released a sigh of obvious satisfaction. "Ah, elixir of the gods." She gestured toward the paper. "Anything exciting in there?"

He hesitated a moment before replying. He hated to ruin her morning as his had been ruined. "I wish you wouldn't have asked me that."

"Why?" She took another sip from her cup and eyed him over the rim.

"There's a story in here that will take that smile right off your face," he finally said.

"What is it?" Her beautiful eyes darkened as she held his gaze.

"There was another killing last night." He told

her what had happened overnight with Greg Bellows and sure enough, any smile that might have curved her lips disappeared.

"This is just what you feared," she said. "This Greg Bellows had nothing to do with the pact."

"Even worse than that is the fact that Greg Bellows hadn't been found guilty of anything. And he didn't murder a person. I mean, I don't believe in any kind of animal abuse, but if Greg Bellows was telling the truth he had no option but to kill the dog. And it was possible he'd just get a fine for the gun charge."

"So the killer is definitely escalating," she replied.

"Yeah." He sighed in frustration. "But with this latest murder happening last night, that means he might not act for another week or so."

"Or he could go back out tonight," she countered. "We just don't know. We're doing all that we can do right now, Jake."

"I know, but it's just not enough."

For the next half an hour they talked murder, and then she went to shower and get dressed for the day.

For the next three days they fell into an easy routine. They went to his job site for about two hours in the mornings and then returned home where he sketched at the kitchen table and she worked on her podcast for that night. At noon they ate lunch together and then at eight o'clock each evening she went back into his office and did her podcast for half an hour. She then returned to the family room where they watched television. Then at eleven thirty they left the house to go watch Adam's house.

The evenings were the most difficult for him, when they sat on his sofa to watch television and all he could think about was the kiss they had shared and how much he wanted to kiss her again.

She made him laugh and she made him feel more alive than he had in years. She was so easy to talk to. They had spent one evening talking about their childhoods and he'd told her more than he'd ever told anyone about the struggles he and Suzanna had encountered as children of addicts.

He had told her about living in squalor and never having enough to eat. There had been end-less seedy motels and even seedier men lurking around.

Child Protective Services had never gotten involved, probably because they were never in one place long enough.

He confessed to her that the times when their mother cleaned up were the scariest times of all, because he and Suzanna had known it wouldn't last. They both knew not to believe or trust that their home life might really get better because it never really did.

Monica made him forget every other woman he had ever dated in his life. Being around her was intoxicating and he was desperately trying to stay sober. The problem was that more and more, she seemed to be attempting to seduce him.

She sat too close to him on the sofa and she touched him often…light and simple touches that nevertheless kept a coil of tension twisted tight in his stomach.

He often felt her gaze lingering on him. He was afraid to return the gaze, feeling as if he'd fall into the depths of her blue eyes and do something really stupid.

This evening was no different, except the tension inside him was at an all-time high. Once again they were seated on the sofa after having eaten a pizza he'd had delivered.

Monica sat close enough to him that he could feel her body heat as her scent filled his head. She'd been quiet all evening, which was unusual.

"Have you spoken with your father today?" he asked to break the silence that had become heavy between them.

"No, why?"

"You've just been really quiet, and I wondered

if maybe you'd spoken with him and he depressed you."

"No, I didn't talk with him today," she replied. She looked back at the television, which was playing some inane comedy show that she hadn't been paying attention to.

She watched television for several minutes and then turned back to face him. "You know what's really bothering me tonight?"

"What?"

Her cheeks took on a pink hue. "Maybe I shouldn't say anything."

"What is it? You know you can say anything to me."

"Forget it," she said, and looked back at the television.

"Monica, what's wrong?"

"Nothing is wrong." She looked down at her hands in her lap and then gazed back at him. There was a bold look in her eyes. "It's just…I can't stop thinking about the kiss we shared."

He stared at her and his breath caught in the back of his throat. "Have you been thinking about it at all?" she asked.

He swallowed hard. "It's crossed my mind a time or two."

"Then why haven't you tried to kiss me again?"

God, she was killing him. He raked his hands

through his hair and drew in several deep, steadying breaths. "Because it wouldn't be fair to you."

She leaned closer to him. "What do you mean? Why wouldn't it be fair?"

He felt as if he was being strangled with his desire for her and she was helping him tighten the noose. "Because I told you before that I don't want a relationship with anyone."

She frowned and didn't take her gaze off him. "But what if we were both on the same page about that? What if I don't want a relationship with anyone, either, and I just want you to kiss me again?"

He tried to look away from her. He desperately fought for self-control. One of them had to be the smarter one in this situation.

Her frown deepened. "Maybe the truth is I'm a bad kisser. Maybe the real problem is you just really don't want to kiss me again."

"Oh, woman, you have no idea how badly I've wanted to kiss you again," he half growled.

She moved so close to him on the sofa she was practically sitting in his lap. "Then kiss me, Jake. I desperately need you to kiss me again right now."

He had the single thought that he was an absolute fool, that they were both complete fools, before his mouth captured hers. Instantly fire leaped into his veins as he tasted her soft, pillowy lips.

She moaned deep in the back of her throat as

she allowed him to deepen the kiss. Her arms rose and her hands moved to the back of his head as she moved closer and closer still to him.

She was so warm and her breasts pressed against him as if to torment him further. Someplace in the back of his mind he knew he should stop this, that he should pull away from her and halt the sweet rush of adrenaline that filled his veins. However, that voice was just a whisper beneath the shout of his desire for her.

She certainly didn't seem inclined to stop the kiss. She moved her hands from the back of his head to his shoulders and actually continued to pull him closer.

He was lost to her, in her.

He couldn't think rationally when he was kissing her. When she was in his arms his brain froze and he was nothing more than his need and want of her.

Finally she pulled back from him. Her eyes appeared to blaze a blue he'd never seen before. He took a moment to breathe.

"Jake, I want you to make love to me."

Her words punched him square in the gut and all the air left his body. All he could think about was having her naked and in his arms. Right or wrong, foolish or not, he didn't want to think anymore.

"Please, Jake." She got up from the sofa and held her hand out to him. "Take me to your bed and make love to me."

He stumbled to his feet and took her hand. "Are you sure?"

"I've never been more sure of anything in my life." Her certainty shone from her eyes and filled her voice.

There were a dozen steps or so where either one of them could have changed their mind about what was about to happen. But neither of them spoke a word as they headed down the hallway toward his master bedroom.

MONICA HAD FOUGHT her growing desire for Jake for what seemed like forever. Kissing him again had only made her want him more. Over the last couple of days the sexual tension between them had been off the charts. And tonight she decided to follow through on that desire.

They entered his large bedroom and the butterflies that danced in her chest had her half-breathless. The only light in the room was the soft illumination that shone from a lamp on his nightstand.

He immediately pulled her back in his arms and took her lips with his once again. His mouth was hot and demanding as his hands tangled in the length of her hair and he held her so close she could tell he was fully aroused.

His mouth left hers and he trailed kisses behind her ear and down the side of her throat. A shiver shot down her spine at the hot sensations he evoked in her. Then once again his lips returned to hers.

It had been a long time since she'd allowed herself to be this vulnerable with any man, and yet something about Jake made her feel safe…safe to explore an intimate moment with him.

She ended the kiss and stepped back from him. Holding his gaze, she unfastened her shorts and stepped out of them, leaving her in the wispy pink silk underpants she'd put on that morning.

She heard his breath catch as his gaze swept down the length of her bare legs. He yanked his shirt over his head and tossed it to the floor.

He had a beautiful chest with well-defined muscles and skin that looked so warm and touchable. His eyes burned with a wildness that only excited her more.

He walked over to her and began to unfasten the buttons on her blouse. She held her breath as he caressed and then kissed each inch of skin that was revealed. When he finished with the last button, he gently pushed the blouse off her shoulders. It fell to the floor behind her.

She watched breathlessly as he stepped back

from her and took off his jeans. He had a beautiful body. His stomach was flat and his hips were lean and his long legs were perfectly shaped.

They got into the bed and instantly their legs entwined as they kissed once again. It was another hot kiss that stirred her desire for him to a new level.

He stroked up and down her back with hands that felt fevered against her skin and she did the same, loving the play of his back muscles beneath her fingers.

His lips slid off hers and once again he trailed nipping, teasing kisses down the side of her neck. At the same time his fingers unfastened her bra. He plucked it from her and tossed it away.

"You are so beautiful," he whispered in her ear. "And I feel like I've wanted you since the moment you barged into my life."

"I feel the same way about you," she said breathlessly, and then gasped as his hands moved to caress her breasts. Then his mouth was there, licking and sucking first one taut nipple and then the other. Electric currents ran through her and her need for him grew.

Within minutes they were both naked and exploring each other's bodies with kisses and touches meant to bring the most pleasure.

It was beyond pleasurable. She was lost in a

haze of sweet sensations. As his hand moved down her stomach to touch at the very core of her, she thought she might explode.

Gently at first, his fingers moved against her in a rhythm that had her gasping. She arched up, needing...demanding more from him. He increased the pressure of his touch and quickened and suddenly she was there, falling over a cliff as wave after wave of pleasure washed through her.

"Yes...oh yes," she cried breathlessly.

For a moment she was limp, boneless in his arms as she attempted to catch her breath. He leaned down and kissed her, the kiss filled with his own hunger.

She reached down and took hold of him. He was fully aroused and he released a deep moan at her touch. Just that quickly she wanted more of him. She wanted all of him.

She stroked his velvety length slowly at first and then more quickly. He moaned again and grabbed her hand to stop her.

He disentangled from her and rolled over to the nightstand. He opened the top drawer and withdrew a condom. She took it from him, ripped the foil and then rolled the condom onto him. For a long moment their gazes locked. She lay back and silently invited him onto her, into her.

He eased into her with a deep sigh and she

closed her eyes as new waves of pleasure shuddered through her. Slowly he began to stroke into her as she gripped his taut buttocks.

She thrust her hips up to meet him, half-wild and out of control. It didn't take long for him to start to stroke faster…deeper, and then she was there again, her climax making her cry out his name.

He stiffened against her and groaned as his own climax gripped him. Neither of them moved; the only sound in the room was their panting breaths slowing to a more normal rhythm.

Languidly she stroked a hand up and down his back. "That was wonderful," she said.

"It was better than wonderful." He kissed her gently on the forehead. "I'll be right back." He rolled off her and then disappeared into the master bathroom.

She stared up at the ceiling and released a deep sigh. She'd half hoped that he sucked in bed, that he would be a selfish or lazy lover. If that had been the case then she'd be over him and she would have easily gotten him out of her head.

But he hadn't been any of those things. He'd been tender and giving and more than wonderful as a lover. Right at this moment, with her body sated and the scent of him lingering on her skin, she knew it was going to be very hard to get him out of her head.

She'd like to stay in bed and cuddle with him, remain in his arms and talk about dreams and hopes and the kind of afterglow conversation most couples indulged in after making love. And that's why she got up.

She was half-dressed when he came out of the bathroom wearing a black robe. He sat on the edge of the bed and gazed at her thoughtfully. "Uh… maybe we should talk about things?" he said tentatively.

"There's really nothing to talk about." She pulled her blouse on and began to button it. "Neither one of us wants any kind of a romantic relationship and nothing about what just happened between us changes that."

She finger-combed her hair and smiled at him. "Let's not make this complicated, Jake. We desired each other, we acted on that desire, and there's nothing wrong with that. We're both single adults. Look at it this way, we're friends with benefits, right?"

He looked relieved. "Okay, then I'll just get dressed and we can go back to television watching until it's time to sit on Adam's house."

"Perfect," she replied, and left him alone in his bedroom. She returned to the family room and sank down on the sofa. She'd talked a good game with Jake just now, but the truth was her heart was starting to get involved with him.

They definitely needed to identify the killer soon so she could get back to her own life and try to forget about Jake Lamont. In the meantime, she definitely needed to hang on to her heart.

Minutes later he rejoined her in the family room but instead of sitting next to her on the sofa, he sank down in his recliner.

"I was just thinking I've been very lax," she said.

He raised an eyebrow. "I would definitely dispute that statement, especially given this evening's uh…activities."

Warmth leaped into her cheeks. "I wasn't talking about this evening. I'm talking about since I've been here. I haven't even called a glass company to get my front window fixed."

"There's no real hurry on that," he replied. "Surely you're not thinking about going back to your house anytime soon?"

"Jake, I need to go home eventually. I'm going to call first thing in the morning and set something up. Would you mind taking me there sometime tomorrow so I can get it done?"

"Just let me know what time and of course I'll take you there," he replied.

They made small talk and watched television until eleven and then drove to Adam's house and parked across the street. Despite the fact that he had just had her in his bed, she was acutely aware of him. His scent…the memory of his touches, just his very presence in the small confines of the car ignited a new flame of desire in the pit of her stomach.

The sex had been amazing, but her desire for him went beyond the actual physical act of love-making. She wanted his arms wrapped around her. She wanted to cuddle with him and press her face in the hollow of his neck where she knew she'd smell his scent. She wanted to gaze into his beautiful eyes and talk about their innermost hopes and fears.

What was wrong with her? The last thing she wanted was an emotional connection with him. Sex was fine, but anything deeper or more profound than that was out of the question.

Their surveillance that night passed uneventfully. He was unusually quiet and she filled the silence chattering about her desire to get a little black schnauzer when this was all over.

The next morning she called the glass company to set up an appointment. "He can't meet us until four thirty this afternoon," she told Jake as they sat at the table drinking coffee.

"We'll be there," he replied.

He'd been a bit distant all morning… quiet and withdrawn. Was it because of their lovemaking? Or was he just tired of having her as a houseguest?

Maybe it was time she really thought about moving back home. While the gunfire that had nearly killed them was still fresh in her mind and the idea of being there all alone was daunting, perhaps she had worn out her welcome here.

They could still do their nightly surveillance, but during the days they'd have their distance from each other.

"I guess the police didn't figure anything out about who shot at us since nobody has called us with any follow-up information," she said, breaking the silence that had built up to be oppressive between them.

"I didn't expect them to have anything for us," he replied. "Drive-by shootings have got to be one of those crimes that are difficult to solve."

"Along with crazy serial killers," she added.

He frowned into his coffee cup and then looked back at her. "I keep thinking there's got to be a more efficient way to out the killer, but damned if I can come up with anything." His frustration was rife in his voice.

She reached out and covered his hand with hers. "We're doing the best we can, Jake."

"I can't go to the police with my gut instincts and without any kind of evidence." He pulled his hand from hers. "I need to stop him before he kills another person."

"So, if it's Adam, then you intend to call the police when he leaves his house in the middle of the night?"

"Monica, it isn't against the law to leave your house no matter what time it is. I intend to follow him to his victim's house and wait until he breaks in, then I'll take him down and call the police."

She stared at him. "Jake, that's way too dangerous," she said softly.

"I told you before I intended to do that," he replied.

"I guess it didn't compute in my brain before. I don't want you to put yourself in that kind of situation."

His eyes were dark. "It's the only way to take down a killer I helped create."

"Jake, you can't take credit for creating a monster. Whether this is Adam or somebody else, they had more than a little bit of monster already inside them before you six got together."

His gaze searched her face. "Do you really believe that?"

"I definitely believe it," she said firmly. "For God's sake, let yourself off that particular hook,

Jake. This person is broken, and was probably broken long before you ever met him."

He leaned back in his chair and released a deep sigh. "I guess I'm just feeling discouraged this morning."

"I'm sorry you're discouraged. What else can we do? Do you want to call the police and tell them you believe Adam is the killer? You don't have to tell them about the pact. You can just say you know him and you believe he's the killer."

He shook his head. "No, I don't want to ruin an innocent man's life and I'm still not one hundred percent sure Adam is our man. It's possible the killer could be Matt Harrison."

"Why haven't you talked much about him before?"

He sighed once again. "Because of all the men, I really didn't want it to be Matt. Matt and I got particularly close when we were attending the meetings. He's my age, and separate from our grief and anger, we had a lot of other things in common. We'd stay at the bar after the others had left and just talk."

"So, what's his story?" she asked.

"His mother was beaten to death by Brian Mc-Dowell. Matt believed that McDowell didn't know she was home when he broke in. She surprised him and he used a baseball bat to kill her."

"Another tragedy," she replied softly. "Brian McDowell was the first victim of the Vigilante Killer.

He nodded. "That's right. Is that a clue? Did the Vigilante Killer murder the man who had wronged him and he then moved on to the others?"

It was a question that hung in the air with no answer. She fought the impulse to reach out and touch him again. She could feel the weight of discouragement wafting off him and she wished she knew how to take it away from him.

He remained quiet through the course of the day and at a little after four they were in his car and headed to her house to meet the glass guy. Jake wore a pair of jeans, a navy T-shirt and another lightweight blazer. She knew beneath the blazer he had on his shoulder holster, which he'd worn each time they'd left the house since the night of the shooting.

"At least with the window fixed the house will be ready for me to come home to," she said as they pulled up in her driveway.

"You're still going to have some work to do on the wall that got shot up," he said. "Don't be in too much of a rush to get back here." He shut off the engine and together they got out of the car.

"You've been so quiet today I thought maybe I'd worn out my welcome."

"That's definitely not the case," he replied. "I guess I have been quiet today, but it's just because I've spent the day trying to see how this all ends and right now I just don't see it.

She withdrew her key from her purse, unlocked her front door, and then turned and smiled at him. "I hope it ends with us being friends long after this is all over."

"I'd like that," he replied.

She shoved her door open but he pushed her behind him and drew his gun. "Let's just check things out before we get comfortable.

She followed him into the dark living room. With the board on the window, it felt like an alien space. His gun led them into the kitchen, where he opened the pantry door to make sure nobody was inside.

Her heart was once again thudding an unnatural rhythm as they left the kitchen and he then led her down the hallway. Was there somebody hiding out in one of her bedrooms? Somebody just waiting for their return here?

He whirled into the first room...her guest room. He walked past the queen-size bed covered in a turquoise spread and right to the closet. He threw open the closet door and then relaxed, but a knot of tension still worked in his jaw.

They cleared the hall bathroom and the room

she used as her office and then approached her bedroom. If anyone was in the house they were somewhere in this room.

Her heart beat more rapidly as they stepped into the room, where the bed was covered with her lavender floral spread and wispy lavender curtains hung at the window. This room had always brought her a sense of calm and peace, but not now.

He checked her master bathroom and then stared at her closet door. There was no sound in the air except for her slightly panicked breaths.

He jerked open her closet door and they both breathed a sigh of relief. "It looks like we're alone," he said, and holstered his gun.

"Thank God," she replied.

Together they returned to the living room, where she quickly turned on one of the lamps on the end table next to the sofa, but even that illumination seemed inadequate to chase away the darkness of evil the room held to her.

Would this ever feel like her home again? Not only did she need to get the window replaced but she also needed to contact somebody about fixing the walls where the bullets had hit. Once all the damage was taken care of, would she be able to embrace this space as her own little haven once again?

"Are you okay?"

Jake's question pulled her from her thoughts. She forced a smile. "I'm fine. It's just that this doesn't really feel like my home right now."

"Once you get things taken care of here I'm sure you'll feel better. Did you contact your insurance company?"

"I gave them a call that first morning at your house. Unfortunately, I have a fairly high deductible so I think these repairs will be out of pocket for me."

"Do you have the money to take care if it?" His gaze turned soft. "I don't mean to pry into your finances, but I'd be happy to help you with this expense."

Her chest swelled with emotion. "Thanks, but I've got this," she replied.

Before she could say anything more, Mitchell Blackmore of Blackmore Windows and Glass and his assistant, a kid named Kurt, arrived. Mitchell and Jake removed the plywood from the window and then Mitchell measured the space.

"I drove by here earlier and eyeballed the window. I guessed at the size, which is fairly common in these homes in this neighborhood, and I have a window that will fit on my truck," Mitchell said.

"Great, then let's get it done," Monica replied.

She sat on the sofa next to Jake, and as Mitchell and Kurt worked to replace the window, the three men talked about sports. Monica fell into thoughts of everything that had happened since she met Jake.

His offer to help her pay for the damage had touched her heart. Heck, everything about him touched her heart. Making love with him had been her idea and she now realized it had been a big mistake. She'd thought she could have sex with him and not get emotionally involved.

She'd been wrong.

She was more than a little bit crazy about him and she hadn't seen that coming. She watched him now as he laughed at something Mitchell had said.

Why didn't he want a relationship? Was it just that he didn't want one with her, or was it that he didn't want to have one with anyone?

Didn't he want a family? Children? They hadn't really talked about these things and now she was curious. And then she told herself it didn't matter what his answers were to those questions. She just wanted her story.

Why couldn't you have your story and your man? a little voice whispered inside her head. She'd always thought that it had to be one or the other. Her career or love. So, why couldn't she have both? She dismissed the very idea. No matter what she felt for Jake, he'd made it clear there was no future with him.

The window was done. Monica paid them with a check and then Mitchell and Kurt left. "Is there anything you need to get from here before we leave?" Jake asked as he got up from the sofa.

She should tell him she was just going to stay here. It would be the smart thing to do. That way she could gain some much-needed distance from him before she fell for him so hard her heart would be scarred forever.

However, she had to admit she wasn't ready to be here all the time and all alone. In fact, she couldn't wait to get out of this place right now. Even with the brightness of late afternoon drifting in the new window, she still felt a darkness that lingered. Maybe in another day or two she'd be ready to return here.

"Yeah, I might grab a few more things." She could use a couple more T-shirts and maybe a few more blouses for her podcasts. It didn't matter what kind of pants she had on because her viewers saw her only from the waist up. But she always wore a professional businesslike blouse when she was being reporter Monica Wright.

"It will just take me a minute or two."

"Take your time," he replied, and sank back on the sofa to wait for her.

She went back in her bedroom and dug a duffel

bag out of her closet and then packed it with the items she thought she might need.

When she was finished she realized she'd packed far more than she needed if she intended to move back here in the next day or two. Oh well, she could always carry it back here when it was time.

She returned to the living room and Jake stood. "All set?" he asked. He reached a hand out to take the duffel bag from her.

"Thanks, but I've got it," she said.

"Okay, then, let's get out of here," he replied.

She locked the front door and they stepped out into the late-afternoon sunshine. She tossed the duffel in the backseat and then slid into the passenger side of his car. He was about to slide in behind the steering wheel when a gunshot sounded and the bullet slammed into Jake's car door.

"Jake!" she screamed.

Chapter Eight

"Get down," Jake yelled at Monica frantically. "Get down and stay down!"

He crouched low behind his car door and looked in the direction from which the bullet had come. Another shot and another bullet slammed into the door. At the same time Jake spied the shooter hiding behind a tree in the distance.

He grabbed his gun and returned fire. Adrenaline spiked through him and his heart beat so fast it felt as if it might explode right out of his chest.

He was vaguely aware of Monica crying, but he had no time to comfort her. His focus was solely on the shooter, who, to Jake's surprise, left the cover of the large tree and began to run away.

There was no way Jake was going to let him get away. This was his best chance to catch and identify the man once and for all.

He stepped away from the cover of the car door. "Jake, no!" Monica screamed.

He didn't listen to her; instead, he took off running after the man. He had a big lead on Jake, but Jake was determined to catch him.

Not only was Jake running all out, but he was also trying to stay close to trees or anything else that might provide cover if the shooter stopped, turned and fired on him.

Yet he half hoped the man would turn around so Jake could get a good look at him. Was he chasing Adam or was it Matt? Both men were built about the same, so he couldn't identify him just from body size alone.

His breaths became pants as sweat rolled down the sides of his face. He fought past the hitch in his side as he raced after the man.

He knew it was the killer. Nothing else made sense and if he could just take him down, then this would all be over. And God, but he wanted it over.

With this thought in mind he pushed himself harder, but the man was apparently running just as fast because Jake wasn't gaining ground on him.

Look back, he willed the person. *Just look back for one minute so I can see your face. Dammit, look back so I can identify you.*

He thought about shooting him and then quickly dismissed the idea. If he shot the man in the back, then he'd probably be the one who wound up behind bars.

The man cut through a yard and quickly climbed over a chain link fence. A dog began barking frantically. Jake followed right behind him, stumbling a bit as he got over the fence.

Another fence rose up before him and he got over it, too. The man disappeared around a corner and when Jake went around the corner as well, the man's gun fired again.

Jake hit the ground. What little breath he had left whooshed out of him. Thank God the man didn't have a perfect aim. Dammit, he hadn't even had a chance to see his face and now he was running once again.

Jake made it to his feet and continued his pursuit.

Once again he pushed himself harder and faster and just when he was beginning to gain some ground, the man jumped into a car parked at the curb and roared off.

"No!" Jake yelled. He instantly bent over at the waist and drew in deep lungfuls of air in an effort to catch his breath. "Dammit." He released a mouthful of curses. He couldn't believe the man had gotten away. He couldn't believe he hadn't been able to identify him.

He turned to head back in the direction of Monica's house. He hadn't even managed to get a license plate number and the dark sedan the man had left in had been completely unfamiliar to him. Neither of the men he suspected of being the killer drove that color car.

He heard a siren coming closer. Monica must have called the cops or perhaps it was one of the people in the neighborhood.

Monica was probably scared out of her mind for him. Or maybe she was terrified for herself, fearing that Jake would be shot and then the man would come after her.

As his car came into view, he saw Monica leap out of the passenger seat and run down the sidewalk toward him. She was crying and when she reached him she threw her arms around his neck. "Jake, thank God you're okay. I was so afraid for you."

"Hey…stop those tears." He swiped her cheeks with his thumbs and then framed her face with his hands. "I'm okay, Monica. We're both okay." He dropped his hands and led her back to his car.

They had just reached it when a police car turned up her street and cut the siren. "I called them," she said. "I… I was so afraid I didn't know what else to do."

"It's all right," he assured her as an officer with a familiar face got out of the patrol car.

"Can't you two stay out of trouble?" Officer

Brian McDonald asked as he approached where they stood.

"Apparently not," Jake replied ruefully.

"So, tell me what happened," he said. "I was called out here because of shots fired."

Monica explained about meeting the glass guy to put in the new window and then Jake took over the story when it got to the bullets flying.

"And you didn't see the man's face?" McDonald asked.

"No," Jake replied in frustration.

"He got into a black sedan?"

"It was either black or dark blue." Jake released a deep sigh. "None of this is going to help you, is it?"

"Not really," McDonald replied. "Is there anyone you can think of who might want you dead?"

"Nobody I can think of," Jake lied. How could he possibly tell the truth about things right now?

"What about you, Ms. Wright? Are you still running those stories about gangs on your podcast?"

"The final one aired last night," she replied.

"Then my advice to the two of you is the same as it was last time I spoke with you. Stay away from here until things have had time to cool off." He looked at Monica. "While I appreciate what you were trying to do with your gang-related reporting, that can be a dangerous world to deal with. It's obvious this guy was sitting on your house and just waiting for you two to return here."

They spoke for a few more minutes and then McDonald waited until they were in Jake's car and pulling out of the driveway before he got into his patrol car and left.

"We both know this had nothing to do with gangs," she said after they had driven a couple of blocks.

"I just wish I'd seen his face." He tightened his grip on the steering wheel as a deep frustration once again swept through him. "Then I would have been sure who the killer is."

"We'll just have to keep sitting on Adam's place until something breaks," she replied. "I was actually thinking about telling you that I was ready to move back to my place before this happened."

"You can move back home when this killer is behind bars," he said, and then realized his voice had been harsher than he'd intended. But the idea of her being in that house all alone right now was untenable. "Sorry, I didn't mean to growl at you, but there's no way I want you alone through this. If I had my way I'd buy you a plane ticket and send you off someplace for a nice vacation."

"And where would you send me?"

"I don't know. Maybe Aspen. You could ski

during the days and then sit in front of a fireplace and enjoy hot rum drinks during the evenings."

"I really don't see myself as a snow bunny," she replied lightly. "And besides, there's no snow in Aspen in August."

"Then I'll send you to a Caribbean island."

"Hmm, I'm not much of a sun worshipper, either. You know, the whole skin cancer thing. I guess this nails it, you're just stuck with me until the very end."

He knew she was trying to lighten the mood, but he didn't want her with him until the end. The gunshot coming out of nowhere had scared him in a way nothing else had. Despite her window being shot out, he hadn't expected a gun. He definitely hadn't expected anything in the middle of the afternoon.

The bullets today were meant for him, but that didn't mean tomorrow there wouldn't be bullets aimed at her. The bad news was the killer probably knew she was a reporter and so she would be seen as a threat.

Nothing was going to change that. Even if Jake was killed, she'd still be a target. The killer didn't want her to talk and tell whatever she might know, just as he didn't want Jake to talk. They both would continue to be in danger until the killer was behind bars. This had gotten far more dangerous than he'd ever thought it would be.

When they reached his house he pulled into the garage and closed the automatic door behind them. Only then did they both get out of the car.

"How does a frozen pizza sound for dinner?" he asked when they were in the kitchen. "I don't really feel like cooking tonight. I've got a meat-lover's in the freezer."

"I don't feel like cooking, either, so that sounds good to me. Can I do anything?"

"No, I've got it." As he turned on the oven to preheat, she sank down at the table. "Beer?" he asked.

"Absolutely," she agreed.

He pulled two beers from the refrigerator and then joined her at the table. It didn't escape him how normal it felt for the two of them to sit together in his kitchen.

It also felt normal for them to sit on the sofa together and laugh about a sitcom or fall into a deep discussion after watching a crime drama. It worried him that he liked her in his house and sharing his life.

He hadn't allowed anyone to get emotionally close to him since Suzanna's murder, but somehow Monica had gotten in. He not only liked her but he believed he was falling in love with her.

And no matter how much he loved her, he couldn't have her.

He had to distance himself from her, but not right now. Despite her chatter, he could feel her fear wafting from her. They had just been through a traumatic experience and now was not the time to pull away from her.

He definitely felt the end coming. He just hoped when all was said and done Monica was safe and sound and could go back to her life with a big story and a few good memories of him.

As THEY ATE their pizza Monica kept up a stream of inane talk. She told him about being a pest to her older sisters when she'd been little and her few memories of her mother when she'd been alive.

"All I remember of my mother is her soft hands brushing my hair away from my face right before she kissed me good-night and the way she smelled of roses and vanilla. Do you have any good memories of your mother?"

"Not really. She was pretty much an absent mother once she started doing the dope. Suzanna and I used to joke that we could be on fire and my mother would use us to cook her stuff."

"That's so not funny," she replied.

"I know. So tell me more about you and your sisters."

"I remember one night my oldest sister and her boyfriend were sitting on our porch swing. I hid in the bushes and watched them because I was sure they would do something scandalous that I could then report back to my father and get her in trouble."

"And?" His eyes held laughter waiting to be released. She loved that look on his face.

"And nothing. They were so boring I fell asleep. I got in trouble for scaring my dad when he couldn't find me anywhere in the house."

The wonderfully deep and warm laugh she'd waited to hear was released from him. She needed the laughter and the talk to keep her fear at bay.

Those long minutes when she'd been sitting in the car all alone and Jake had gone running after the bad guy had been the most torturous she'd ever experienced.

She hadn't been afraid for herself; rather, all of her fear had been for Jake. She was terrified that he'd be hurt and she couldn't imagine the world without Jake in it.

And in that intense fear for him, the depth of her love for Jake had been realized. It didn't matter that they'd known each other only a short amount of time. It didn't matter that the timing wasn't right for her to be in love. The truth of the matter was she was in love with him and timing be damned.

Now she had to figure out what she intended to do about it. Right now she wanted to deal with none of it. She just wanted to laugh and eat and relax after the harrowing afternoon they'd had.

"Then there was the time I put a frog in my sister's bed," she continued, wanting to make him laugh again.

"I'm sure that didn't go over well," he replied.

She gave him a slightly wicked grin. "I can still hear her screams in my head. Sadly I was grounded for a week. When my dad asked me why I would do such a thing, I told him she acted like she was a princess, so I thought if she slept with the frog he'd turn into a prince who would take my sister to his castle."

He laughed again. "You must have been something else. I almost feel sorry for your sisters."

"Oh, trust me, they deserved everything I did to them. They were both mean to me when we were all young. When I was nine they had me convinced that I was adopted and Mom and Dad had taken me in because nobody else in the whole world wanted me."

"So, you never got close to them when you got older?" he asked.

"No. I think a lot of the problem was they were so much older than me. They had different interests than me and we just never really connected.

I love them both and we get along fine when we get together for holidays. We just never really became friends."

"Maybe it isn't too late to change things with them," he replied. "I'd love to have more siblings. Wouldn't your sisters be the keepers of your mother's memory?"

She looked at him in surprise. "I never really thought about it that way before." There had been several times in her recent memory that her sisters had invited her to lunch, or to coffee, and she'd always come up with an excuse not to meet them. When this was all over maybe it was time for her to do things differently when it came to her sisters.

She continued to chatter as they finished the pizza and cleaned up the kitchen. After dinner they moved into the living room and turned on the television. It was then that the fear she'd suffered while waiting, while wondering if Jake would return to the car, began to simmer once again inside her.

He sat close enough to her that she could smell the comforting scent of him; she could feel his body heat radiating toward her.

She'd thought he might not return to the car when he'd taken off after the gunman. She'd been so afraid he'd be shot and fall to the ground and die before anyone could get to him.

As these dark thoughts continued to fill her

head, she moved closer to him. Emotion permeated her chest and tears pressed hot at her eyes.

"Monica, are you all right?" he asked.

She turned and looked at his beautiful face and the tears that had only burned at her eyes began to fall. "No…no, I'm not okay," she managed to say. "I… I think I'm having some kind of stupid delayed reaction."

"A delayed reaction about what?" His gaze was soft, but obviously bewildered.

"I was just so afraid for you when you took off running after the gunman." Her emotions were spiraling out of control and at the moment she couldn't do anything about it. The tears chased each other down her cheeks as a choking sob escaped her.

"Hey, hey," he said softly, and then he did what she wanted him to do more than anything in the world…he drew her into his arms.

She clung to him as her tears continued to fall and she was grateful that he held her so tightly that she could feel the reassuring steady beat of his heart.

His arms warmed every cold place in her body and she welcomed the warmth. They also offered strength and the assurance that he really was okay.

At this moment her getting her story seemed unimportant. What was important was that Jake survive through this. It was important that he keep building beautiful structures that inspired people. He needed to continue to live and breathe and laugh until the natural end of his life. And she'd like to live that long, wonderful life with him.

Her tears slowed and finally stopped. Reluctantly she pulled back from him and gave an unsteady laugh. "Sorry about that. I don't want you to see me as a big crybaby."

"I don't, and I'm sorry you were so frightened," he replied.

"I really was. All I could think about was you being wounded and lying all alone in somebody's yard."

He smiled at her. "I feel like we're a couple of old cats who have nine lives."

"What scares me is I think we've already used up several of those lives," she replied.

He sobered and held her gaze. "Monica, there's no reason for you to use up any more of those cat lives."

She shook her head to stop anything else he was about to say. "We've already had this discussion more than once and there's no point in having it again. I'm in this until the very end."

He frowned. "You're extremely stubborn."

She grinned. "Yes, I am, and you should remember that."

"So noted."

They returned to watching television. But she was still deep in her thoughts. Without her fear, there was nothing to stop her from thinking about her feelings for him. She began to nibble on her fingernail.

"I thought you were trying to stop that," he said.

She gave him a sheepish smile and dropped her hand back to her lap. "Thanks for reminding me. I'd like to have pretty nails, but I can't achieve that if I don't quit chewing on them. It's a nervous habit I need to stop."

"Are you nervous right now?"

"Not really," she replied.

As they continued to watch television, her thoughts were all over the place. When had her emotions toward him gone from liking him to loving him? Had it been when he'd released his last burst of laughter? Or when he looked at her with that soft, warm gaze that made her feel like the most important woman in the world?

Had she fallen from like to love the first time he'd kissed her? Or had it been when he'd told her about his sister and she had shared his pain?

She didn't know the answer. All she knew was that despite her desires to the contrary, she was in love with Jake Lamont. And she believed he had feelings for her, too.

When the show they had been watching ended, she turned to look at him. "Jake, why don't you want a long-term relationship in your life?"

The question obviously took him by surprise. "I just don't."

"Do you mean right now you don't want one or you never want one for the rest of your life?"

"I intend to be alone for the rest of my life," he replied. Tension had straightened his shoulders and his eyes became dark and hooded.

"Don't you eventually want a family? Maybe children?"

He leaned forward and raked a hand through his hair. "I thought about it at one time," he answered after a long pause. "But then I changed my mind."

He looked achingly sad. She placed her hand over his. "Was your change of mind because of Suzanna's murder?"

He hesitated once again and then gave a curt nod of his head.

"Oh, Jake. Do you really think that's what Suzanna would want for you? To be alone for the rest of your life?"

"It doesn't matter what she'd want. She isn't here and this is a choice I've made for myself," he replied. He pulled his hand from beneath hers.

"Then it's a choice that makes me very, very sad for you," she replied softly.

"Don't be sad for me. I'll be fine. I have my work and that's all I need."

"Work doesn't keep you warm on a cold night."

"When my bedroom gets cold, I just turn up the heater," he replied.

"Work doesn't make a good conversationalist," she countered.

"I like talking to myself just fine," he answered flippantly. "Besides, you've said the same thing, that you don't want a long-term relationship."

"That's just for right now. Eventually I do want a family. I want to be married and have two children. I want to wake up in the morning and see a man who loves and adores me every morning across the kitchen table. I want to sleep in the same man's arms every night until I die. I can't imagine that you wouldn't want that same thing for yourself."

"Well, I don't."

She released a deep sigh. The conversation was going nowhere and she knew for sure now wasn't the time for her to confess that she was in love with him. That definitely wouldn't make the remainder of their time together comfortable.

It was funny…a couple of weeks before she would have been arguing that her work was enough, that she didn't need or want any relationship to take her mind off her ultimate goal of success.

But what really defined success? Was it a thousand more blog followers or looking at the same man across a dinner table for the rest of your life? Was it getting the big story or was it having somebody who wanted to share the little moments of your life with you?

All she hoped for right now was that somehow before this all came to an end, Jake would decide he wanted love and a long-term relationship in his life and she desperately hoped he'd realize he wanted that with her.

Chapter Nine

It had been an awkward conversation the night before and the next afternoon Jake found it playing and replaying through his mind. He sat at the kitchen table with a sketch pad before him, but the last thing on his mind at the moment was building designs.

All he could think about at the moment was the warmth of Monica's body in his arms while she'd cried with her fear for him. When he'd told her he intended to live his life alone, her beautiful blue eyes had radiated sadness…and something else… something that had made his breath catch in the back of his throat.

For a moment he'd thought he'd seen love shining true and strong from her eyes. He didn't want her to love him. Dammit, she was supposed to just want her big story and nothing more from him. Her loving him would only make telling her goodbye that much more difficult. And he had every intention of telling her goodbye when this was over.

Once again they had spent a couple of uneventful hours of the night staking out Adam's house. They had both been quiet during those hours and he'd been grateful to get home and go to bed.

Unfortunately his sleep had been filled with visions of her. In his dreams they had been sitting on a metal beam, staring up at the stars overhead, and then they had been in his bed and making love. He'd finally awakened with a bittersweet longing for what he couldn't have.

She was now in his office, doing research for the podcast she did every night at eight. He never told her but when she was doing her podcast from his office, he was usually in the kitchen watching it on his laptop.

She always looked professional clad in dress blouses, although beneath his desk where the viewers couldn't see she was in shorts and sandals.

Her takes on the news stories of the day were different and thought-provoking. She offered the viewers human-interest stories that were sometimes funny and sometimes sad.

Once she left his house and they returned to their own private lives, he would never watch her again. It would be too painful to see her on the air every night and remember her time here with him.

She'd told him that she hoped they would be friends at the end of all this and he'd agreed that would be nice. But he realized now he couldn't be her friend. When this was all over he had to completely cut her from every aspect of his life.

He'd pray for amnesia where she was concerned. He'd open up all his doors and windows to rid the house of her exotic scent and make sure not an article of clothing of hers remained behind when she left here.

There was no way he'd want to meet her for a friendly lunch or for coffee. When they said their final goodbyes, he needed to somehow never think about her again.

He looked up as the object of his thoughts bounced into the kitchen. "Guess what?" She sat at the table facing him, her eyes sparkling brightly.

"What?"

"My snitch just called me. He said earlier this morning some man walked into the North Patrol station and confessed to being the Vigilante Killer and they're taking his claim very seriously."

"Did he tell you who it was?" Jake sat up straighter in his chair as a burst of adrenaline filled him. Was it possible? Would the killer really turn himself in?

"No, he said he'd call me with more details as soon as he could." She leaned forward, a simmering energy wafting from her. "Do you think this could really be the end?"

"I don't know. The guy taking shots at me yesterday didn't seem to me to be the kind of man who would suddenly develop a conscience and feel remorseful enough to turn himself in," he replied dubiously. "But I suppose anything is possible," he added. "Did he give you any indication when he might get back to you?"

"I got the impression it wouldn't be that long. He said things were popping very fast on the case."

"Who is this source of yours?" he asked curiously.

"He's a lieutenant at the North Patrol."

"And how did you get hooked up with him?" he asked. "Did you show up on his front porch, too?"

She laughed. "No, we dated for a while in high school and remained good friends after we broke up."

"Is this somebody who still might have a thing for you?" He wasn't sure why he held his breath waiting for her to reply.

"Heavens, no," she said with another laugh. "In fact, he married one of my best friends and they have a four-year-old and a new baby."

He didn't want to examine the wave of relief that shot through him. She obviously had him twisted up in his brain. "So I guess we just have to wait until we have more information," he said.

"Even though this wouldn't exactly be a big and dramatic end to a story, him turning himself in would be the best way for this to end for everyone," she said.

"As long as he can't kill another person, that's all I've ever cared about," he replied. Right now he had too many questions to feel confident that this was really the end. It just seemed strange that the perp would decide to give up and turn himself in.

"But I'm sorry that it sounds like you won't get your big story…unless you decide to go public with everything I told you about the murder pact. Now that would probably be the kind of sensational story you want."

She stared at him with eyes that suddenly held a touch of frost. "I would hope you knew me better than that. You told me that information in confidence and I would never run with that story. It offends me that you even entertain the idea that I might."

She continued to stare at him, apparently waiting for him to offer her some sort of an apology. But he remained silent. Maybe it was a good thing she was irritated with him. If this really was the end of things, then maybe making her a little angry with him wasn't all bad.

"I'm going to go check and see if any other newscasts have this as breaking news," she said, and jumped up from the table. "I'll let you know if I get more information." Her tone of voice held the frost in her eyes.

He watched her leave the kitchen and then he stood and walked into the family room. He was now too restless just to sit. Instead he paced back and forth in front of his sofa as thoughts whirled around in his head.

He was sorry if he'd hurt Monica's feelings, but maybe that's what he needed to do. Maybe he needed to show her that he was a miserable man who deserved to be alone.

Thoughts of Monica were overtaken by thoughts of the latest development. Once again he wondered if it was possible this really was the end. That the killer had turned himself in. Even though he found it hard to believe, he hoped like hell it was true.

He and Monica would no longer be in any danger. There would be no more heinous deaths of people with Vs carved into their foreheads and Jake would be able to finally put this all behind him.

And it would be time to tell Monica goodbye for good. He was surprised at the wave of depression that swept through him at this thought.

He needed to tell her goodbye, but that didn't

mean he wouldn't miss her smiles and the sound of her laughter. He'd miss her chatter and even her grumpy face in the mornings. He was just going to miss her like hell.

Fifteen minutes later she joined him in the living room where he'd finally sat in his recliner and turned on the television. "I checked every news source I could think of and nobody is reporting anything on the killer." She sank down on the sofa with her cell phone in hand. "I'm just hoping my snitch will let me know what's going on sooner rather than later."

She gazed at him for several long moments. "If this really is the end of things, there's one thing I want us to do before I go back to my house."

"What's that?" he asked tentatively.

"I want you to take me up in the beams and show me Suzanna's stars."

Myriad emotions rushed through him. Memories of his sister…his love for Monica…and the pain of a final goodbye to both. For a moment he couldn't speak as a huge lump rose up in the back of his throat.

"I'm sorry. Maybe it's not such a good idea after all," she said.

"No, I think it's a great idea," he finally said. He'd take her up to the stars and then he'd send her back to her house, back to her life, and he would return to his life of isolation.

As they waited for her to get another call from her snitch, he channel surfed to see if they could find any breaking news about the killer. But there was nothing.

He glanced over at her and noticed she was chewing on her fingernail once again. "Nails," he said.

She dropped her hand to her lap. "Thanks."

"Have you always been a nail-chewer or is it something you picked up when you met me?" he asked half-teasingly.

"Unfortunately, I've always been a nail-biter, but there's no question that the more stress I'm under the more I chew. What bad habits do you have that I haven't seen yet?"

It was a silly conversation considering they were waiting to get more information about a serial killer, but during their time together he realized she not only chewed her nails when she was stressed, but she also chattered.

"Socks," he replied.

"Socks?"

He nodded. "I have a bad habit of taking them off at night and leaving them at the foot of the bed instead of throwing them in the dirty clothes basket. Sometimes I have three or four pairs at the end of the bed before I pick them up."

"Thank goodness," she replied.

He quirked an eyebrow. "Thank goodness?"

"Yes, thank goodness you aren't as perfect as I thought you were. You do have some flaws."

"Trust me, I'm far from perfect," he replied. If she only knew how imperfect he was, she'd probably run for the hills.

"There's got to be more than socks," she said, her eyes holding a teasing light. "Do you leave the top off the toothpaste? Or maybe when you refill a toilet paper roll you do an under instead of an over?"

He laughed. "Is that really a flaw?"

"Definitely," she replied, and then laughed. "I can't believe we're talking about a serial killer and toilet paper."

"You started it."

Her laughter faded as she stared down at her cell phone. "I just hope he calls soon. I feel like my nerves are jumping out of my skin waiting to find out if this guy who turned himself in is for real."

"I feel the same way. I'm just hoping he's really the killer.

"If he is, then I don't have to worry about you doing something stupid." She held his gaze.

"What do you mean? I try never to do stupid things."

"Your plan to take this guy down while he was in the act of committing murder was a stupid and reckless idea."

He frowned. "It was a plan to get him under arrest once and for all."

"It was a plan that put you at deadly risk," she replied.

"I'd still do it if it meant getting this guy off the streets once and for all."

"You're very stubborn," she observed.

"Yes, I am, and you'd do well to remember that," he said teasingly.

"Duly noted," she replied, parroting his response about her stubbornness.

Fifteen minutes later she got a call from her friend, who told her there would be a news conference at four o'clock that afternoon, and that's all the information he had for her.

Would they learn the identity of the man who had confessed during the press conference? Had Matt or Adam walked into the police station and turned himself in?

Waiting was a study in torture. Monica went back to Jake's office to work on her podcast for that evening and he once again found himself pacing restlessly as he waited for the news conference. He hoped this was the end. This had been a burden on his soul since the very first murder. He couldn't even imagine how he would feel if that particular weight was finally lifted.

It didn't escape him that a new burden had been carved into his heart, and that was his feelings for Monica. When she left, there was no question she'd leave a huge hole and memories of what life might have been like if he'd made a different decision on the night of Suzanna's murder.

At four o'clock they were both back in the living room and seated on the sofa with the television tuned to a local channel that would broadcast the news conference.

A red banner appeared at the bottom of the picture, announcing breaking news. On the screen a lectern appeared and police officers began to fill the space. Chief of Police James Donahue stepped up to a lectern.

James Donahue was a popular man in Kansas City. He was a big man with a burly chest and a head full of snow-white hair. He was beloved not only by the officers who worked beneath him, but also the people of the city. He was known as a straight shooter who didn't give a damn about politics.

"I'd like to begin by introducing the officers who have been working around the clock on the

Vigilante Killer case. When I call your name please step forward. Detective Chuck Baker..."

As the officers were called forward, Jake glanced over at Monica, who was chewing on her index fingernail as she leaned forward and watched the television. "Nail," he said softly.

"Right," she replied, and dropped her hand to her lap.

"This morning a man walked into the North Patrol and turned himself in, claiming he was the Vigilante Killer," Donahue said. "After questioning this individual at length, we believe he is who he claims to be."

Reporters began shouting questions. Donahue held up in his hands in an effort to quiet everyone and then he continued, "The man is forty-year-old Grant Timmons and we are still determining motive. That's it, folks. I am not taking questions at this time."

He left the lectern with reporters shouting questions. The channel went back to regular programming and then a local reporter came back on screen with an interview with one of Timmons's coworkers.

"Of course we were all stunned to find out about Grant, but we also knew he seemed to be struggling a bit in his personal life. He lost his parents in a car accident about three months ago and he wasn't the same after that." The reporter spoke to the man for another few minutes and then regular programming returned. Jake lowered the volume on the TV.

It wasn't Adam and it wasn't Matt. Jake was positively stunned.

"Grant Timmons. Do you know him?" Monica asked.

Jake frowned. "The name doesn't ring a bell."

"Let me see what I can pull up about him on the computer," she said, and jumped up off the sofa.

"My laptop is in the kitchen. Why don't you bring it in here?"

As she went to retrieve the computer, he racked his brain for any memory of a Grant Timmons. If he really was the killer, then why had he killed the perps of the men who had been in their murder pact? Why had he come after him and Monica? It didn't make sense.

Monica returned with the laptop and placed it on the coffee table before them. Her fingers danced over the keys and within moments she had a picture of Grant Timmons pulled up.

The photo was on a law firm site where Grant was listed as a paralegal. Jake leaned forward and studied the picture of the dark-haired man.

"He looks vaguely familiar," he said slowly.

"Is it possible he went to the Northland Survivor Group, too?" Monica asked.

"Maybe. I'm thinking maybe he sat in the meetings and never interacted with anyone. We had several men who never introduced themselves or spoke at the meetings. But I can't be sure that the guy I'm thinking about and this Grant are the same person."

"Surely the police wouldn't come out publicly and name the subject without vetting the story," she said.

She was right. The authorities had to have found some kind of corroborating evidence that proved Grant Timmons was, indeed, the Vigilante Killer. Otherwise they wouldn't have held that press conference.

Thank God he hadn't said anything to the police about Matt or Adam. If he had he could have potentially ruined the life of an innocent man.

"So I guess it's really over," he said. "I'm sorry you weren't the one to break the big story."

She shrugged. "There will always be another story at another time. I'm just glad the killer is behind bars and you and I don't have any bullet holes in our body."

"That is definitely a good thing. So, I guess since we don't have to do our middle-of-the-night surveillance we can go star-watching tonight to celebrate."

"I can't wait. And then tomorrow morning I guess I'll pack up my things and move back home." She looked at him as if waiting for him to say something, anything, that would change things.

But he couldn't choose to change his future. It had been decided for him on the night he'd made a selfish choice that had resulted in the brutal death of his sister.

It was a beautiful, clear night and at midnight Jake came out of his bedroom wearing jeans, a T-shirt and one of his black blazers.

"Are you wearing your gun?" she asked in surprise.

"I am."

"But with the killer behind bars surely we don't have anything to worry about."

"It's just a precaution. I'm not thinking about the Vigilante Killer, but I am thinking maybe I should have it with me just in case the drive-by shooting at your house was either the work of gang members or even Larry Albright."

"I don't think it was either of those. I can't help but believe it was the work of the killer."

"But why? Why would he go after the two of

us? We weren't anywhere close to outing him. Neither of us knew him."

She held his gaze and frowned. "I don't know. I don't think we'll ever know the answer to that question, but I guess the gun is a good thing. It doesn't hurt to be prepared," she replied.

"My thought exactly. Besides, when I go downtown at this time of night I always carry."

Minutes later they left his house for his job site.

Although she was looking forward to the night activity of stargazing, overall she was depressed. It wasn't the loss of a big story that had her disheartened; rather, it was the loss of something she'd thought would be wonderful, something she'd somehow thought would happen with Jake.

She'd believed he might be in love with her. She'd thought she'd seen it in his gaze and felt it in his touches. She'd tasted it in his kisses and yet he hadn't said anything to stop the plan of her going home in the morning. And she'd given him a perfect opportunity to do just that.

That upset her far more than not getting the story. She couldn't believe how much she'd changed, how her priorities had shifted since Jake had come into her life.

When they had first met, they had been just alike in their assertions that work was enough, that they didn't want or need anything else in their lives. She was still passionate about her work, but she also had a passion to have Jake in her life forever.

"You're very quiet," he now said, pulling her from her thoughts.

"I've just been thinking about everything that has happened since I so rudely shoved my way into your life," she replied.

He flashed her a quick grin. "It's definitely been a wild ride."

"Definitely," she replied. She'd been kissed and shot at, she'd feared for Jake's life and her own, and through it all she'd fallen in love.

"How often did you and Suzanna go stargazing?" she asked. She needed talk to keep her brain off the emotions that were far too close to the surface.

"Not that often. Maybe once every six weeks or so. It always depended on the weather and the cloud cover and how busy we were with our personal lives and what building was in a state to allow us to go up in the beams," he replied.

"Tonight looks like a perfect night. There isn't a cloud in the sky."

"That's supposed to change. Storms are supposed to move in sometime before morning."

"Then thank goodness we didn't wait any later to come out, and hopefully we'll have time before anything moves in." She looked out the passenger window. The houses they passed were dark and there were few cars on the road.

It was nice to know they were on their way to see nature's beauty and not going to spy on a man they thought was a killer.

She turned to look at Jake, loving the way the dash light illuminated his handsome features. There was a faint five o'clock shadow on his jaw and it only added to his attractiveness.

"Will this be painful for you?" she asked softly.

"What would be painful?"

"You're taking me to a place where you always took your twin sister." She watched his features closely and relaxed when a soft smile curved his lips.

"When we get up there, will I remember times spent with Suzanna? Absolutely. But they will be good memories about her life."

"And when we get up there, I want you to share more of Suzanna with me." For a moment she wondered if she'd pushed him too far, but he smiled once again.

"I'd like that."

They rode the rest of the way in silence. She released a soft sigh. Her heart was going to be completely crushed when she packed up her things and left his house in the morning.

It wouldn't be because she didn't want to go home; rather, it was because his house had become her home. She didn't want her time with him to end. But he'd never wavered from his declaration that his desire was to spend his life alone.

She'd been such a fool to allow her emotions to get so tangled up with him. Still, there was a tiny nugget of hope in her heart that when tomorrow morning came, he'd confess that he was in love with her and ask her to stay with him forever.

Dammit, she hadn't imagined him falling in love with her. She hadn't misread his soft glances, the caring touch of his embraces and the desire that still simmered between them like unfinished business. She knew in her heart he was in love with her. What she didn't know was why he would deny himself her love.

When they reached the job site, Jake parked and they both got out of the car. She looked up at the huge skeletal structure silhouetted against the night sky and lit slightly by the streetlights in the area.

"Seeing it in the daytime and at night are two very different things," she said.

"I guess it could be seen as being a bit scary at night," he agreed.

She wasn't about to admit to him how nervous heights made her. She didn't ride the Ferris wheels at carnivals and she'd never chosen to go to a lookout point that was a cliff hanging in the air. But she believed she'd be fine as long as he was by her side.

"We'll go up to the sixteenth floor. The beams on that floor are about two feet wide," he said.

Two feet wide? Twenty-four inches wide? That didn't sound so reassuring. "Isn't there a floor where the beams are at least six feet wide?" she asked.

He laughed. "Afraid not." In the moonlight that spilled down, his features were visible. His smile fell away, and he reached out to shove a strand of her hair away from the side of her face.

There it was… She could swear it was love pouring from his eyes, in his gentle touch. She leaned toward him but he dropped his hand to his side and stepped back.

"You know, we don't have to do this. We can just go back home and call it a night," he said, as if he'd accurately identified the faint fear that whispered through her as she thought of going up on the beams.

"No, I want to do this, but I will admit I have this little thing about heights. As long as you promise me I won't fall, then I'll be fine."

"I promise you'll be fine," he assured her. He took her hand in his and led her to the cage that would take them up. Before they started the ascent, he helped her with putting on a safety harness and then he put one on himself. "I also promise this will be a wonderful experience for you."

As the cage began to take them up, he pulled her close to him. "Can you hear my heartbeat?" she asked.

He smiled at her. "No, I can't hear it. Is it racing?"

"Like a horse at the Kentucky Derby."

"You just tell me if and when you want to go back down and we will."

"I'm sure I'll be fine once I get up there," she replied. As they continued upward she kept her gaze on him, refusing to look down to the ground below.

Just looking at him and feeling his arm around her eased most of her fear. This was a man who had saved her life when bullets had flown through her front window. He'd tried to talk her out of partnering with him a dozen times because he was trying to keep her safe.

If he thought this was dangerous then they wouldn't be doing it. He would have never put his sister in danger, either. Monica knew without doubt that he would never willingly put her at risk. Knowing this took away any lingering fear she might have entertained.

When they reached the sixteenth floor they stopped, and before she stepped out of the cage, he hooked her harness onto a safety line that ran waist-high across the beam. He then did the same for himself.

"Ready?" he asked. He pulled a flashlight out of his coat pocket, hooked it onto his belt loop and clicked it on.

"I think so."

"I'll go first and if you want to hang on to my shirt or whatever, then you can. We'll take it slow and easy and then stop when we get about midway across."

Midway looked like a long ways away as she stared across the narrow steel beam. "And you swear this safety line will hold me if the worst thing happens and I misstep and fall? You know I've put on a few pounds since I've been staying with you."

A low rumble of laughter escaped him. "Honey, these safety lines work for men three times your size, even if you have put on a few pounds. You ready?"

"Yes, I'm ready." She drew in a deep, steadying breath.

As he began to walk across the beam, she followed right behind him, her hand holding on to the back of his shirt. Thankfully he took small steps.

When they reached about the halfway mark, he turned toward her. "I'll help you sit."

He steadied her while she sat, her legs dangling into dark nothingness. When he sank down next to her, she immediately placed a hand on his thigh, needing to touch him in order to stay grounded.

There was a bit of a breeze that smelled clean and fresh, but held a faint scent of approaching rain. Up here the skies looked different than they did on the ground. The stars looked so much bigger and brighter without the effect of city lights dulling their brilliance.

"Whatever possessed you and Suzanna to do this in the first place?" she asked.

"It was actually Suzanna's idea. She wanted to be closer to the stars and so she talked me into going up in a building we were working on at the time."

Monica looked out and up. "I definitely feel closer to the stars up here. It's beautiful."

"Yeah, but I see a few clouds creeping in."

"Hopefully we'll have plenty of time for you to point out all of Suzanna's favorite stars to me before any storm moves in," she replied.

"I'm not sure she had a favorite." He pointed. "Can you see the Big Dipper there?"

She followed his finger and spied the constellation. "I see it."

"Suzanna used to say the Big Dipper held all the rainbows and occasionally those rainbows would spill over and fall to the earth."

"That's beautiful," Monica said. She couldn't help it, she felt so close to him at this moment she grabbed his hand in hers. "I think I would have liked your sister."

"I think she would have liked you, too," he replied. "You probably would have been good friends."

"I don't have many friends right now. I've been so focused on my work I've kind of neglected all the friends I once had."

"Maybe it's time you rectify that," he replied.

"Maybe. What about you? Do you have friends?" During the time she'd stayed with him, she didn't think he'd received any calls except business ones.

"No. All the friends I once had went away while I was going through my grief and rage period. I pushed them all away."

"Maybe it's time you rectify that." She echoed his words back to him.

"I really don't want to rectify it. I'm good alone."

Once again her heart broke for the wonderful man seated next to her. He was a man who laughed easily, a man who appeared to love life, and yet he intended to live only half a life.

For several moments they both gazed up. "Oh, did you see that?" she exclaimed. "A shooting star."

"I saw it." His voice was soft. "Suzanna used to say that shooting stars were the souls of people who have been released from purgatory and are now on their ascent to heaven."

She squeezed his hand as she heard the deep emotion in his voice. She had a feeling for some reason Jake was trapped in his own purgatory. She just wished if that was the case, that he'd find his way out before she was forced to walk out of his life in the morning.

Chapter Ten

For the next half an hour Jake continued to point out the various constellations in the sky. He was vaguely surprised by how many he remembered Suzanna teaching him about.

He was also surprised that thoughts of Suzanna didn't evoke the piercing, agonizing grief anymore, but instead just brought up a deep and profound sadness that he would never be able to spend time with her again.

Even though he was sharing Suzanna's stars, most of his thoughts up here belonged to the woman who sat next to him and held his hand.

If things were different he could have easily imagined a life with Monica. She enchanted him with her humor. She challenged him with her intellect and she humbled him with the love he felt radiating from her to him.

It was possible she might be brokenhearted when she left his house in the morning, but she'd get over him. Even though he'd jokingly told her he had no skeletons in his closet, he had lied.

Eventually she would find a good man who truly had no skeletons, a man who could love her with open arms and an open heart. But that man wasn't him.

"Was Suzanna always into the stars, or was it an interest she developed as an adult?" Monica asked.

"I think it all started when she was about ten and I bought her a poster that showed all the constellations. I tacked the poster on the ceiling above where she slept. Whenever we moved I made sure the poster always came with us."

He paused thoughtfully. "We never knew where we would live or when we'd get our next meal. Sometimes we were awakened in the middle of the night to sneak away from a landlord my parents owed money to. With all the chaos of our childhood, me and the stars were the only real constants in her life."

"You shame me," she replied.

"How so?"

"I complain that my father doesn't respect my work and I don't believe he loves me as much as I'd like, but I always had a beautiful bedroom and woke up in the same house every morning. I always had food and heat and water and I can't imagine what horror you and your sister went through as children."

"Unfortunately we don't get to pick our parents," he replied.

She squeezed his hand. "I would have picked far better parents for you and your sister."

"Thanks. But that all seems like a lifetime ago."

"So, are you already dreaming of the next building you'd like to see or have you been commissioned by somebody to build another one?"

"I've had a developer contact me about another project, but we're just in the talking stage. It's a smaller office building up north. I'm sure in the back of your brain you're always working on a story for your podcast."

"I thought I had my big story, but that's all fizzled away. I know there will always be another story."

"I still find it hard to believe this man turned himself in. It just doesn't seem to be characteristic of that particular killer."

"I can't imagine the police doing that press conference without having corroborating evidence," she replied. "But I don't want to talk about killers, I want more talk about stars and hopes and dreams."

And that's what they did. He talked to her about his ideas for buildings that would transform the modest skyline of Kansas City into something magical. "We're never going to be a New York or San Francisco, but there's no reason why we can't make the skyline here something people talk about," he said.

She then talked about wanting to be the reporter Kansas City looked to for local stories and news they could trust. "I like going beyond the stories and talking to the people who are affected by crimes. That's why initially I wanted you on my podcast."

He chuckled. "You were rather tenacious. I couldn't believe it when you turned up at my house."

"I'm not sure I would have done that if I hadn't gotten the information about you attending those meetings."

They fell silent for several minutes. The breeze had picked up a bit and cooled off. Thoughts of his sister flitted through his head. He was confident Suzanna would have approved of him bringing Monica up here to see the stars.

Yes, he was certain Monica and Suzanna would have been great friends. They both shared a zest for life and a great sense of humor.

"Have you ever thought about living someplace else?" she asked, pulling him out of his thoughts.

"Never," he replied easily. "This is my home-town and I love it here. What about you?"

"Same. I think this is a great city to live in and I've never wanted to live anyplace else. It's not only a great place to live but I think it's a great place to raise children."

There was part of him that never wanted this time…these moments with her to end. Unfortunately the clouds had begun to thicken, the cooler breeze had begun to blow, and he thought he heard a distant rumble of thunder.

"I think it's time for us to head down," he said reluctantly. "It looks like a storm is moving closer and this is the last place we want to be if it starts to lightning."

"Okay, but there's just one more thing I need to say to you," she replied.

A new tension wafted from her and he knew instinctively he didn't want to hear what she was about to say. What little moonlight was left shone on her face and bathed her features in a silvery glow as she gazed at him.

"I'm in love with you, Jake."

He stared at her in dismay, wanting her to take back the words that had just fallen out of her mouth. From the corner of his eye he caught a movement. He gazed past her and froze.

Matt Harrison stepped out of the cage, a gun in

his hand. And there was only one reason he would be here. The police had gotten things wrong.

Adrenaline spiked through Jake's body. In an instant he made a decision... He shoved Monica off the beam. She screamed with terror as she went flying down below the beam and into the darkness.

Jake got to his feet and grabbed his gun. With the other hand he clicked off his flashlight, knowing that it would make him more of a visible target if it was on.

"Matt, what are you doing here?" he yelled above Monica's panicked screams. Jake was sorry about what he'd just done to her, but at least with her dangling in the air below the beam and not between the two men, she wasn't an immediate and easy target.

"You know why I'm here. You're weak, Jake," Matt yelled back.

Monica finally grew silent and he wondered if she'd passed out with fear. "What are you talking about?" Jake asked.

"You know what I'm talking about. You broke the rules by working with that reporter. Have you told her everything? Is she going to break a big story and out me? Have you told her about our murder pact?"

"What murder pact?" Monica screamed from out of the darkness. "Nobody told me anything about a murder pact." Jake drew a breath of relief, knowing she was okay. "Jake is my boyfriend and I don't have any idea who you are or why you're bothering us."

Jake's hand tightened on his gun as a flight-or-fight tension overtook him. Only there would be no flight. He couldn't run from this, especially knowing that Monica wouldn't be safe. But he wouldn't have run even if she wasn't here.

This was what he'd wanted. The ability to stop the killer. It pained him that it was Matt and that the man was now here to continue a reign of terror.

"Matt, what are you doing? I thought we were good friends. Why don't we all get down from here and go someplace where we can have a beer together and really talk?" He didn't want to have to kill Matt. What he'd like to do was talk Matt into turning himself in.

"We were friends, Jake, but that all changed when you hooked up with that reporter. I'm not letting you take me down."

"I don't want to take you down. I want you to turn yourself in and get some help." A flash of lightning split the sky, followed by a rumble of thunder. "Come on, Matt. Let's go have a few beers and then I'll go with you to a police station."

"You don't understand, Jake. I have a calling

now. It's my moral duty and job to kill all the guilty people in this city."

"Did you shoot out Monica's front window?" Jake inched backward on the beam.

"Yeah, that was me. You two have been a bit of a problem when it comes to killing you." Matt didn't move from his position. Jake suddenly realized that apparently the man had been so eager to get to them he hadn't put on a safety harness and wasn't tied into the safety line.

Jake continued to inch backward, so that he was next to an upward beam. "Matt, this isn't a calling. It's a sickness. I think something broke inside of you when your mother was killed."

God, Jake didn't want to shoot Matt, especially knowing even if he only wounded him the man would probably fall to his death. He didn't want Matt dead; he wanted him arrested.

He didn't want to be killed by Matt, either. If Matt managed to kill him then he would surely kill Monica as well, and Jake couldn't let that happen.

"Damn straight something broke inside me," Matt screamed, his voice filled with rage. "She was a saint, Jake. My mother was such a good, loving mother. She was a God-fearing woman who volunteered at a homeless shelter and that piece of crap beat her to death. I have nightmares about the pain and suffering she endured in those horrific moments before her death. This is my job, to rid the world of creeps, and you know what the best part is? I like it. I like it a lot and nobody is going to stop me."

In another flash of lightning, Jake saw his intent. Jake jumped behind the beam as Matt fired his gun. Monica screamed once again.

Lightning once again split the sky as Jake leaned out and fired on Matt. He missed and Matt laughed. It was the hysterical laughter of a man who had lost touch with reality.

"God is speaking, Jake. Don't you hear him in the thunder? He's telling me that I'm his warrior on earth." Matt fired his gun once again.

Sirens whooped in the distance. Had somebody heard the gunfire and called the police? Jake would gladly tell them his role in this if it meant getting Matt off the streets.

Still, even if the police arrived they couldn't exactly get up here and place Matt in handcuffs. There could be a hundred cop cars parked below them and they would be no help in this situation.

Ultimately only one man was going to come down from here. It was either going to be Jake or Matt. If it was Matt who survived then he prayed Monica would be able to tell the police enough to get him arrested.

The sirens grew closer and the thunder and

lightning added to the chaos of the standoff between Jake and Matt. "Matt, the police are coming. You need to turn yourself in," Jake yelled in a final attempt to end this without anyone getting hurt.

A bullet ricocheted off the steel column behind which Jake was hiding. It was obvious to him that Matt had no intention of turning himself in.

Several more shots sounded and Monica screamed once again. Jake's heart stopped. Matt was now firing on Monica. She screamed and then moaned and then her screams stopped, and there was nothing but the thunder and the lightning and Jake's terrified rage. Had she been hit? Oh God, was she dead?

Not caring for his own safety, driven only by his fear for Monica, he stepped out from behind the column. Half-blinded by the rain that had begun to fall and his own tears, he fired his gun over and over again.

MONICA CAME TO SUDDENLY. Her upper arm hurt like hell and a steady rain had begun to fall. From somewhere Jake was calling her name over and over again.

She still dangled in the air, a breeze buffeting her hanging body. She realized that her fear of heights and the pain in her arm had apparently made her pass out. What had happened? Where was Matt?

"Monica," Jake cried. His voice was filled with desperation.

"Jake?" she finally answered.

"Oh, thank God. Are you okay?"

"No, I'm not," she replied, and a sob caught in her throat. "I want to get down. Please get me down from here, Jake. I just want to go home."

"I'm going to pull you up to me," he said. "And then I promise I'm going to take you home."

She looked down to the ground, surprised by a half a dozen patrol cars that shone their bright searchlights up to where they were.

Where was Matt? Had he gotten away? Was this not the end but rather the beginning of a new cat-and-mouse game? She moaned as the pain in her upper arm intensified as Jake began to pull her up to the beam where he now stood.

It wasn't until they were both in the cage that she collapsed against him. "Where's Matt?" she asked.

"Dead." Jake pulled her closer into his arms and then gasped. "Oh my God, you're hurt."

She followed his gaze and was shocked to see blood running down her arm. "I… I think I was shot. It hurts, but I'm okay." She pressed closer to him. "Are you okay?"

"I am now. I... I thought you were dead. I thought he'd killed you." Emotion was thick in his voice. She looked up at him and she couldn't tell if his cheeks were wet because of the rain or because he'd been crying.

When they reached the ground the police were waiting. "She needs medical attention before we talk to anyone," Jake told the man who had identified himself as Sergeant Ben Wallace.

"I have a dead man on the ground and I need some answers," the sergeant replied.

"She's been shot. Right now that's more important to me than a dead man on the ground," Jake said gruffly.

He didn't leave her side as she was led to an awaiting ambulance. He stood by silently as the medical team cleaned the wound. Thankfully it was only a graze. She was bandaged up and then they were ready to speak to the officers, and Monica wasn't about to let Jake incriminate himself in any way.

"The dead man is Matt Harrison, the real Vigilante Killer," she said. "Jake met him in a grief group and had some suspicions about him. He came to me with those suspicions and we were trying to find out if those concerns were true. Tonight he tried to kill us to keep his secrets safe."

The two of them were taken to a nearby police station where they were questioned for hours. Jake said nothing about the murder pact, but he did say that there were six men who had become friends during their meetings at the Northland Survivor group.

They had been in the sergeant's office for about two hours when another officer walked in to tell them a search warrant had been executed and in Matt's house they had found evidence that supported the fact that Matt was the serial killer Monica and Jake claimed him to be.

It was nearly dawn when they were driven back to the job site and Jake's car. "It's finally for sure over," she said in exhaustion.

"And now you know it was all Matt…no gangs and no Larry Albright. Matt did it all."

"I'm just so tired I feel like I could sleep for a month," she replied. She stared out the passenger window, where lights had begun to appear in homes as people got out of bed and readied themselves to face another day.

Even though she was tired, there was still a streak of residual fear that had a grip on her. Although it was over, she had a feeling it was going to take her a while to put this night behind her.

She turned back to look at Jake. "I've never been as scared as I was when you shoved me off that beam. Swinging in the air sixteen stories high was terrifying."

He grimaced. "I'm sorry. It was the only way I knew to make you less of a target. Unfortunately, it didn't completely work. How does your arm feel?"

"It hurts, but not too bad. I'm sorry you had to kill a man you considered a friend."

"Yeah, me, too. But when he started shooting at you I saw red and I knew he had to be stopped immediately. He was so busy shooting at you he didn't see me shooting at him." He released a deep sigh. "It's been a hell of a night."

That was an understatement. They didn't speak again until they reached his house and walked in through the front door. "I think we could both use at least a couple hours of sleep," he said.

"I definitely second that," she replied. Her eyes itched with tiredness, and a slight headache had begun to pound across her forehead. Her arm hurt and it was going to take some time for her brain to unscramble and process everything that had happened.

"I'd say you have a pretty riveting story for your podcast tonight. You not only helped in identifying the killer, but you were shot by him and survived. You've got your big story, Monica."

"Maybe I'll be excited about the story later after

I've slept. Right now I'm just too exhausted to care."

"Then I'll just say good-night for now," he said.

Together they went down the hallway where she went into her room and he walked on down to his. She peeled off her clothes and pulled a nightshirt over her head. She then went into the bathroom and washed her face and brushed her teeth.

Minutes later she was in bed, but the minute she closed her eyes she was flying in the air…in the dark…with nothing to hold on to. Gunshots echoed in her head and fear closed up the back of her throat and iced her body.

She gasped and opened her eyes. Fear still pounded through her veins and she knew she'd never get to sleep in this bed by herself.

She needed…she wanted…Jake. Without any other thought in her mind, she got out of bed and walked down the hallway to his bedroom.

He was in his bed, covered up by a sheet, and his eyes were closed. "Jake?" Her voice trembled.

His eyes opened drowsily and he looked at her. "What's wrong?"

"Nothing, but can I…can I sleep in here with you?"

He held her gaze for a long moment and then raised the sheet, a silent invitation for her to join him. She moved quickly across the room and slid into the bed.

He immediately pulled her back against his chest and his arm went around her waist. His warmth took away the ice inside her. The strength of his embrace comforted her.

Her last thought before she fell asleep was that neither of them had mentioned the fact that just before Matt had appeared on that beam, she'd told Jake she was in love with him.

Chapter Eleven

Jake woke slowly, and instantly all his senses came alive with Monica. Her soft curves were tight against his body and her scent surrounded him.

He'd been asleep for about two hours. Monica was still soundly sleeping in his arms. He knew he wasn't going to go back to sleep, but he remained in the bed anyway.

He'd love to wake up like this every morning for the rest of his life. She fit so perfectly against him, as if she had specifically been made for him. He'd definitely love to have her in his arms all night long for every night he had left on this earth and then wake up each morning and see her across the breakfast table from him.

But that wasn't going to happen. What was going to happen was that this was probably going to be one of the worst days of his life. It was the day he had to tell her goodbye.

He drew in the scent of her and remained perfectly still, wanting to savor these last moments with her in his arms. He wished things were different. He wished he were the kind of man who could welcome her love with open arms. He wished they could get a black schnauzer and have a couple of children and live happily ever after. But that just wasn't going to happen.

With this thought in mind, he eased away from her and out of bed, grateful that his movements didn't wake her up. He grabbed clean clothes and then padded down the hall to the guest bathroom. He didn't want to shower in his own bathroom where the sound of the water might disturb her.

When she'd appeared in his bedroom doorway and had asked to sleep with him, he knew it had been residual fear that had driven her into his arms for the last time. One thing he had learned about her was that she tended to process events long after they happened, and then she got emotional.

Standing beneath a hot spray of water, he felt as if he needed to scrub himself clean of the scent of her and wash away the feel of her body against his.

When he was dressed, he went into the kitchen and made a pot of coffee. It was a gray day. It was as if the dark clouds from the night before had decided to stick around and might at any moment spit down more rain. The gray day mirrored the condition of his heart.

He poured himself a cup of coffee and then moved into the family room, where he turned on the television and searched for any news stories concerning the events of the night before.

While everyone was reporting on the death of the serial killer, nobody had the story of the life-and-death struggle that had taken place high on the beams of the building. Monica would be able to report that story.

However, the news reports did let him know Grant Timmons had been released from custody. He was not the killer, but he was a troubled man who had professed to be. There was no question that there had been a rush to justice where he was concerned.

He and Monica were both mentioned, him as a respected architect and her as a podcast reporter. She would be pleased by the publicity the news would generate for her. She was definitely going to gain new viewers.

Several reporters spoke about the issue with Grant Timmons, finding it inexcusable that the police had trotted him out at a news conference before fully investigating him. The reporters called for an investigation into the release of Grant's name.

Then there was Matt.

A picture of him appeared on the television with

the reporter talking about the murder of his mother and the evidence police had found in his home. It not only included a hit list of sorts, but also pictures of his victims taken right after their murders and tacked to Matt's bedroom wall.

Pictures… Jake's mind couldn't comprehend that the man he had once considered a friend got up every morning and went to bed every night with pictures of the heinous murders he'd committed on his bedroom wall.

Jake turned off the television and went back into the kitchen and sat at the table. He didn't need to see any more news. What he needed to do was prepare himself for telling Monica goodbye.

I'm in love with you, Jake. Her words whispered over and over again in his head. It was the last thing she'd said to him before he'd shoved her off the beam.

He hoped he didn't hear them again today. Dammit, he'd warned her from the very beginning that he wasn't interested in any meaningful or lasting relationship. Even after they had made love she'd indicated they were both on the same page and it hadn't meant anything emotional between them.

He released a deep sigh and swallowed hard against his own emotions as he thought about what the rest of the day would bring once she woke up.

Walking down the hallway toward his bedroom, his mind told him to go back to the kitchen, but his heart wanted just a moment to gaze at her while she was unaware.

She was curled up facing him as he stood in the doorway. Her hair was a silky spray of darkness against the white pillowcase. He'd never seen her animated features at rest. She looked peaceful and achingly beautiful. Her eyes were closed and her long dark lashes dusted her upper cheeks. Her mouth was slightly open, as if awaiting a lover's kiss.

He clenched his fists, stepped back from the doorway and then went down the hallway to the kitchen. He poured himself another cup of coffee and once again sat at the table to wait for her to wake up.

An hour later she walked into the kitchen. Clad in her navy robe and with her hair tousled, she looked as beautiful as he'd ever seen her. His heart squeezed tight.

As usual she beelined to the coffee and poured herself a cup and then sat at the table across from him. A sleepy smile curved her lips. "It seems odd to say good morning at this time of the day, but good morning." She raised the cup to her lips and took a deep drink.

"Back at you," he replied. "Did you get enough sleep?"

"For now."

"We made the news."

"Tell me all."

While she drank her coffee, he told her everything he'd learned from listening to the various news reports on television. All the while he talked to her he was already starting the grieving of her absence.

There would be no more shared coffee in the mornings or cuddling on the sofa in the evenings. He would no longer hear the sound of her laughter or see the tiny frown line that occasionally danced between her eyes when she was thinking.

By the time he'd finished telling her everything he had heard on the various news reports, she had finished two cups of coffee. "I'm going to go take a quick shower and get dressed." She stood. "I'll be back in just a few minutes."

When she left the room he cleaned up the coffee cups and then went back into the living room. Rain had started to patter against the windows.

He stared out the window and a knot of tension twisted in his chest; it was tension based in grief. This would be the second time he'd had to tell a woman he loved goodbye. He would never, ever put himself in this position again.

He was still standing at the window when Monica came in the room. She was dressed in a pair of jeans and a deep blue T-shirt that made the color of her eyes pop.

"Let me know when you're ready to pack up your equipment and I'll help you," he said.

She didn't move. She stared at him with an intensity that threatened his breath. "Please, don't send me away, Jake."

"It's over, Monica. It's time for us each to go back to our own lives." The pain of his words reflected in the blue depths of her eyes.

"But it doesn't have to be over." She took several steps toward him. "Jake, did you not hear what I said to you last night? I'm in love with you."

He stiffened his shoulders and tried desperately to erect a mental defense against her. "I'm sorry, Monica, but that changes nothing."

She took another two steps forward, now standing so close to him if he leaned forward he'd be able to capture her lips with his.

And heaven help him, that's what he'd like to do at this very moment. He wanted to draw her against him and take her mouth with his. He needed to tell her that he never wanted her to leave, that he needed her to be here with him forever. But he did none of those things.

"I believe you're in love with me," she said softly.

He shook his head. "I'm sorry if I gave you that impression. I thought we were both on the same page and knew that when the killer was no longer a threat, we'd go our own separate ways."

"I believe we're still on the same page." She now stood so close to him he could smell not only her dizzying perfume, but also a minty scent from her toothpaste. "Jake Lamont, you look me in the eyes and tell me you aren't in love with me."

He couldn't do it. He couldn't lie to her. "It doesn't matter what I feel or what you feel." He desperately tried to hang on to his emotions, but he already felt them slowly spiraling out of control.

He stepped back from her and sought anger rather than the killing pain that caused hot tears to press behind his eyes. "Dammit, Monica. I warned you that I intended to live my life alone. I warned you that I didn't want love in my life."

"But why? Tell me why you don't want love. Don't you want to grow old with a partner? Do you really not want any children or a family…a safe place to fall in a world of chaos?"

"Monica, please don't make this any more difficult than it already is." He hadn't expected her to fight him…to fight for him.

"I'm not trying to make it difficult, I'm trying

to understand. I love you and you love me so why does this have to be so complicated? Why does this have to be the end?" Her features were taut with both pain and confusion. "Surely after everything we've been through together I deserve an answer," she added softly.

"You know what the answer is?" The guilt that he'd carried around for two long years came crashing down on him. "I don't deserve any happiness or laughter or love in my life because I'm the reason why my sister was murdered."

MONICA STARED AT HIM. His entire body trembled and his shoulders slumped forward. His eyes misted with tears and he looked like he was on the verge of a complete breakdown. "What are you talking about?" she asked softly. "Max Clinton murdered your sister."

"She would have never been at her house that night if I hadn't been so damned selfish." Tears trekked down his face and he swiped at them angrily. "She was murdered because of me."

"I can't imagine you doing anything terrible, Jake."

A bark of laughter escaped him. "Really? Maybe you just don't know me well enough to realize what kind of man I am."

"What kind of selfish thing do you think you

did on the night your sister was murdered?" She reached out to touch him, but he brushed her away and took several steps backward. "Tell me, Jake. Tell me what happened that night."

He collapsed on the sofa, as if his legs wouldn't hold him any longer. He dropped his head in his hands. When he looked back up at her, his eyes were nearly black with torment.

"Even though it had been two months since the last time Suzanna had spoken to or seen Max, she still believed he was stalking her. She'd go to work every day but when dinnertime rolled around she'd show up here and she stayed every evening here, more times than not falling asleep on my sofa."

He raised his head and looked beyond her shoulder. His voice was flat and weary as if he'd gone over this a million times in his mind. And in replaying it, someplace along the line he'd broken.

"That night I was tired of her company and I had a date. I wanted to bring my date back here and I didn't want a pesky sister hanging around."

Monica sank down next to him but knew instinctively now wasn't the time for her to touch him in any way. He was lost in the memories of that night "I made her leave. I knew she didn't really want to go, but I kicked her out of the house anyway." For a few moments he didn't speak as tears fell down his cheeks. His grief and guilt were painfully palpable in the air.

She finally broke the silence. "What else did you do?"

He looked at her in surprise. "That's it. Isn't it enough that I kicked her out of a place where she would have been safe and placed her right in the arms of the man who killed her?"

"Oh, Jake." She sighed and then did what she wanted to do. She placed her hand on his forearm. "You're going to hold yourself responsible for the rest of your life because of this? Because you were human and wanted a night to yourself?"

He started to pull his arm away from her, but she held on tight. "I made it possible for Max to kill her."

"Max wanted her dead and if not then, he would have found another time and another place. He was the monster, Jake…not you."

Her heart ached for him. He'd carried around this guilt, this sense of responsibility for his sister's murder, for two long years. And apparently he intended to carry it with him and punish himself for the rest of his life unless she could change his mind. And she desperately needed to make him realize he was in no way responsible for his sister's murder.

"Jake, let yourself out of the prison you've put

yourself in," she said fervently. "You did nothing wrong." Tears of frustration burned at her eyes as she felt his resistance in the tense muscles of his arm.

"This isn't what Suzanna would want for you. She wouldn't want you to turn your back on love and happiness. She wouldn't want you to live your whole life alone. Please, Jake. Tell me I can stay. Tell me you want to build a real life with me."

He looked at her and in his eyes she saw a sadness that made the tears chase faster and faster down his cheeks. "Monica, I'm sorry."

He pulled his arm from her grip and stood. "Let me know when you're ready to pack the car and I'll drive you home." He turned and walked out of the room.

She remained on the sofa as sobs of heartache ripped through her. She couldn't believe this was how it was going to end. For several long minutes she remained seated, hoping and praying that he would come back into the room and tell her he'd changed his mind.

When that didn't happen she drew several deep breaths to stop her tears and rose from the sofa. Now all she wanted to do was get to her own house, where she could truly cry for what might have been.

It took her almost half an hour to pack up all

her clothes and toiletries, and as she worked a curious numbness swept through her. She then went into his office and packed up all her equipment. She carried or dragged all the suitcases and duffel bags to the front door.

During all this Jake remained in his bedroom with the door closed. The coward. He'd destroyed her and then had run to his bedroom to hide from the emotional fallout.

She strode down the hallway and knocked on his door, a tiny flame of anger igniting in her chest. "I'm ready," she said when he opened the door.

He gave a curt nod and followed her to the front door. Neither of them spoke as they loaded her things into his car. They also didn't speak on the drive to her house.

She played and replayed what he'd told her and the flame of anger burned just a little bit brighter. He'd taken on the responsibility for Matt Harrison's actions and intended to carry the burden for Suzanna's murder for the rest of his life.

When they reached her house they silently unloaded everything into her living room and then he stood by the front door apparently to say a final goodbye.

"You're something else, Jake," she said as she allowed her anger to rise to the surface. "You must think you're some important person in the grand scheme of life. You alone unleashed a killer and you somehow believe you're responsible for your sister's murder. You know what I think?"

His eyes had become dark and hooded as he met her gaze and his features were stoic, as if he was going to allow her to vent and then he'd just leave.

"I think you're a big coward. I think you're hiding behind tragedies so you don't have to face real life and real love. You're a big coward, Jake Lamont."

"Monica," he said softly.

She raised a hand to silence anything he might want to say. Tears began to blur her vision. "I don't want to hear anything you have to say unless you're going to tell me you love me and want a life with me."

"I never meant to hurt you," he replied.

"You're hurting yourself way more than you're hurting me. In the last couple of weeks I've realized that I want love in my life. I love my work, but I want more. I wanted that with you, Jake."

A sob caught in her throat. "I know you love me, Jake. I didn't imagine your love. I know it's real and true and I think what we had…what we could have would be beyond wonderful. But you're too big a coward to handle it. You've made it clear to me that you're too scared to take a chance on love. You're going to wear a damned safety line through the rest of your life and that will keep you safe from any emotional ties you might build."

Another sob escaped her and suddenly her anger was gone, replaced by a wild grief. "Please Jake, don't make me beg for you. Look deep in your heart and tell me you want me as much as I want you." She stopped and bit her lower lip as she saw his answer in the darkness of his eyes.

Without another word she turned and headed down the hallway. When she reached her bedroom she heard the sound of the front door closing.

He was gone.

Chapter Twelve

Monica sat at her table drinking her morning coffee. It was a few minutes after ten and even though she had just gotten out of bed, she was exhausted. Her arm hurt but that pain didn't begin to compete with her wild heartache.

She'd cried for hours yesterday after Jake had brought her home. She'd half hoped he would magically reappear and tell her he was ready for her love, but that hadn't happened. She had only managed to pull herself together about an hour before her podcast. For the first time the podcast was difficult for her.

As she'd told her viewers about the terror of being up on the beams when confronted by a serial killer, all she could think about was Jake. When she'd reported about them being shot, her heart had cried for her man.

Somehow she had managed to get through the podcast and then had collapsed in bed. She'd cried herself to sleep, but thankfully she'd slept without dreams. However, the minute her eyes had opened, thoughts of Jake assailed her once again.

He was right. He had warned her, but the heart knew what the heart wanted. And despite her intentions to the contrary, her heart wanted him. And what really broke her was that she knew with every fiber of her being that Jake loved her.

He was the fool. A misguided fool who planned on keeping himself isolated from others because of a guilt he shouldn't own.

She'd hoped her love might heal him. She'd definitely hoped he would pick love over his guilt, love over fear, but that hadn't happened.

With a sigh she got up and poured herself another cup of coffee. Later today she intended to contact somebody to fix the Sheetrock in the living room. She needed to reclaim her house as a safe haven and she couldn't do that until the bullet damage was gone.

Maybe she should just let the damage remain. When she looked at it, her thoughts would always take her back to the night she and Jake had shared their first kiss, the first night he had saved her life.

No, she was going to get the wall repaired or replaced and then maybe she'd paint the entire room a new color to go with a fresh start.

Her doorbell rang. Every muscle in her body

froze. Jake? Was it possible he'd changed his mind about things? She jumped up from the table, her heart beating wildly in triple time.

She ran to the door. She unlocked it and flung it open. All the joy that had momentarily filled her whooshed out of her. "Dad, what are you doing here?"

"Aren't I allowed to visit my daughter? Hmm, I smell coffee."

"Come in and I'll make you a cup." She opened the door wider to allow him in and wondered what had really brought him here.

Neil Wright was a big man, with big arms from working construction all his life. He'd retired a year ago and Monica was glad he now had a life of fishing and golfing.

He went into the kitchen and sat at the table. "I watched your podcast last night."

She popped a coffee pod into the machine and then turned and looked at him in surprise. "You did?"

"Yeah, to tell the truth I've watched you several times, but I don't want you ever to put yourself in danger like you did with this Vigilante stuff. You're good at this reporting stuff, but you don't have to put yourself in dangerous situations to get a story."

She stared at him. He'd just told her she was

good, words she'd been waiting to hear from him, but she hadn't been good enough for Jake. She suddenly burst into tears.

"Hey, hey." Neil got up from the table. "What's going on here? For God's sake, why are you crying?"

She shook her head, unable to answer him with the raw emotions that had a grip on her.

To her surprise he pulled her into his arms as she wept uncontrollably. He patted her back awkwardly as she cried into his broad chest with his big arms encircling her.

She couldn't remember the last time her father had held her in his arms. She cried for a few minutes and then raised her head and looked at the man who had raised her. "He broke my heart, Daddy. Jake broke my heart."

"Give me his address and I'll go beat the hell out of him."

His mock bluster made her laugh. She swiped at her tears as he released her. "Sit back down and I'll get the coffee."

Moments later the two sat across from each other. "You have no idea how much I've wanted to hear you say something positive about me," she confessed.

He looked at her in surprise and then leaned forward in his chair and gazed at her thoughtfully. "Maybe I haven't been good at letting you know how proud I am of you. Your sisters were so easy to raise. They're both just like your mother. They're natural pleasers. But you, you scared the hell out of me. You were so much like me. You were a rebel and you questioned everything. You were a real challenge to raise, but honey, I've always loved you and I'm always proud of you. You just never seemed to need me as much as your sisters."

"I really, really needed to hear everything you just said to me," she replied. "I really needed to know that you love me."

Neil frowned. "I'm sorry. I didn't know. When your mother passed, I was terrified. I was suddenly the single parent to three little girls. You know, there wasn't a manual to tell me how to do it."

"You've been a great father. Maybe I should have asked for what I needed from you."

He smiled at her. "Once and for all, I love you, Monica. I love you with all my heart."

He leaned back in his chair. "Now, enough of this emotional stuff. I see you have a bandage on your arm. How is that doing?"

Monica's heart swelled with the words her father had spoken to her. They were what she'd wanted...what she'd needed to hear from him for years. And she had a feeling she would never hear them again.

"Dad, you have to respect that doing the podcast is my career. It's what I want to do."

He frowned. "I understand that, but you can't blame me for wanting the best for you. Last night when I heard what happened to you, it scared the hell out of me. I can respect what you do and still want you to be safe and financially secure."

"I seriously doubt I'll ever be in a position again to face a serial killer."

"I hope not. I know you and your sisters aren't close, but before I die I'd like to see that change. They are your family, you know."

"They don't seem to want a relationship with me," she replied. "They just ask me out for coffee and stuff because they feel obligated."

"I think you're wrong. They care about you, Monica."

They talked for about a half an hour and then he left. If nothing else came from this, at least she felt a new closeness to her father.

But with him gone there was nothing left except her heartbreak. Half a dozen times throughout the day she thought about calling Jake.

But what for? To ask him if he'd changed his mind about them? If that had happened, then he would be here with her right now. She wasn't going to beg for his love.

Around two she decided to take a nap. She'd gotten little sleep the night before because she hadn't been able to stop crying.

She immediately fell asleep and into dreams of Jake. And in those dreams she was in his arms and he was making sweet love with her. Then they were sitting at his kitchen table and laughing together. Finally they were walking down the sidewalk with a double stroller in front of them. In the stroller was a little dark-haired girl and a little dark-haired boy. Twins.

She awakened crying for all she would never have with the man she loved. She had to get back her excitement, her wild passion for her work, and stop thinking…somehow stop loving Jake Lamont.

Over the next five days the news cycle changed and stories about the serial killer were few and far between. Her podcast subscribers grew in number and she told herself she was fine. She saw her family doctor, who rebandaged her arm and prescribed some antibiotics.

A cool front had moved in and suddenly it felt more like fall than summer. She packed away some of her lightweight things and pulled out sweaters and blankets. She gathered two bags of clothes and shoes to donate. Two men spent two days fixing the Sheetrock in her living room and then she spent an afternoon painting. She went shopping for new pictures to hang on the wall and kept up a frenetic pace that gave her little chance to think.

She managed to convince herself she was fine until the long, dark hours of the night. She sometimes felt as if he were haunting her. She imagined she could smell him in her sheets and feel the heat of his body warming hers.

She kept telling herself it was just going to take more time for her to forget Jake. But each day she awakened with the same heartache of what might have been.

This morning she had decided to scrub the kitchen from top to bottom. She needed to clean out her pantry and wash down tiles. She threw on a pair of jean shorts and an old navy T-shirt and then drew her hair up in a messy ponytail.

The only way she had gotten through each day was to stay busy. She didn't want to give herself time to think because her thoughts always ended up on Jake. And those thoughts always brought on another bout of tears.

Another good outcome of the big story of the killer was that both her sisters had called her, offering their love and support. She'd made plans to meet them for lunch the following week. She might have lost at love, but she'd gained a new relationship with her family.

She started scrubbing the tiled area behind her sink with a lemon-scented cleaner. As she worked she tried to stay focused on her podcast and what she intended to report that night. There weren't a lot of stories that had really captured her and begged her to dig deeper.

With school starting in the next couple of days, tonight she had a taped interview from a security expert talking about school safety.

A knock on her door pulled her from her work. It was probably her father stopping in for coffee. He'd mentioned on the phone the day before that he might come by again.

She yanked open her door and a small gasp escaped her. Jake. "Can I come in?" He looked like he hadn't slept in weeks. Lines of exhaustion ran down the sides of his face and there was a hollow darkness in his eyes.

She opened the door to allow him in. Why was he here? She steeled her heart against him. He didn't look like a man who had come here to profess his love for her; rather, he looked like a tormented man.

"The wall looks nice," he said when he entered the living room. "I like the new color."

"I know you didn't come here to check on my

home repair. Why are you here?" Her heart beat a faster rhythm as she gazed at him.

He sank down on the sofa and released a deep sigh. "From the moment Suzanna was murdered I decided that I would be alone for the rest of my life. It had always been her and me against the world, and without her I was utterly lost."

Monica sat on the chair facing the sofa. Was he here to clear his soul? Did he feel the need to once again go over all the reasons why he couldn't return her love? Was he here to once again reject her? She said nothing but continued to gaze at him.

"You were just supposed to stay a partner in finding the killer. You were never supposed to be anything else."

"Why are you here, Jake?" she asked again. Seeing him again was killing her. This might be something he felt like he needed to do, but she couldn't just sit here while he told her all the reasons he couldn't be with her.

"I'm here because you were right. I've been a coward. I was afraid to face life. My grief over Suzanna made me afraid to care about anyone else again. Intellectually I know that I'm not responsible for her murder, but it was easy to grasp on to that to keep people away."

He stood and walked over to her. He took her hand in his and pulled her up out of the chair.

Her heart quickened its pace as she gazed into his eyes…eyes that now held warmth.

"I thought I'd get over you. I thought I could push you out of my house and out of my heart. Monica, these past five days have been the longest in my life. All I could think about was what a fool I was. I watched your podcast each night and longed for you."

"You longed for me? Tell me more." She knew now why he was here and joy filled her heart. But as much as she loved him, as much as she wanted him, she also wanted him to grovel a bit. He owed her a little groveling after the five long days of grief he'd put her through.

He reached up and stroked her cheek with his thumb. "I missed seeing your cranky face across the kitchen table each morning. I missed hearing your voice and smelling the scent of you. You're right—Suzanna wouldn't have wanted me to live my life alone. I want you, Monica. I need you. Please tell me I'm not too late, that you're still in love with me." He dropped his hand to his side and his eyes burned with a fierce intensity as he gazed at her. "I love you, Monica. For heaven's sake, tell me you'll come home with me and be my wife… my partner through life."

For a moment she couldn't answer. Her joy, her

happiness, was too big for words. She nodded and then a laugh escaped her. "Yes," she finally said.

He pulled her into his arms and kissed her long and deep. She tasted his love for her. She felt it in his strong arms that surrounded her.

When the kiss ended he stepped back from her. "Wait right here," he said, and then he went back out the front door.

What now? She stood staring at the door, waiting to see what was going on. Jake came back in, and in his arms was a small bundle of black fur. Two black eyes gazed at her curiously.

"Her name is Cookie. She's eight weeks old and as you see she's a black schnauzer. I figured taking care of her would be good practice for when we have kids."

"Oh, what a sweet baby," she said as she took the puppy into her arms.

"I want kids, Monica. I want a family and a dog and I want it all with you," Jake said.

"We'll have it all, Jake." The puppy barked as if in agreement. Monica laughed. As Jake took her lips once again in a tender kiss that spoke of their future, she knew this was the best story of all, a story that ended with love and laughter and puppy kisses.

* * * * *

*Don't miss these suspenseful stories in this
series by New York Times bestselling author
Carla Cassidy:*

Desperate Strangers
Desperate Intentions

INTRIGUE

Available June 18, 2019

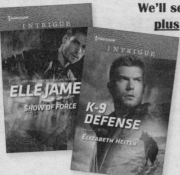

*One night, when Mary Cardwell Savage is lonely, she
sends a letter to Chase Steele, her first love. Little does
she know that this action will bring both Chase and his
psychotic ex-girlfriend into her life…*

Read on for a sneak preview of
Steel Resolve *by* New York Times *and* USA TODAY
bestselling author B.J. Daniels.

The moment Fiona found the letter in the bottom of Chase's
sock drawer, she knew it was bad news. Fear squeezed the
breath from her as her heart beat so hard against her rib
cage that she thought she would pass out. Grabbing the
bureau for support, she told herself it might not be what she
thought it was.

But the envelope was a pale lavender, and the handwriting
was distinctly female. Worse, Chase had kept the letter a
secret. Why else would it be hidden under his socks? He
hadn't wanted her to see it because it was from that other
woman.

Now she wished she hadn't been snooping around. She'd
let herself into his house with the extra key she'd had made.
She'd felt him pulling away from her the past few weeks.
Having been here so many times before, she was determined
that this one wasn't going to break her heart. Nor was she
going to let another woman take him from her. That's why
she had to find out why he hadn't called, why he wasn't
returning her messages, why he was avoiding her.

They'd had fun the night they were together. She'd felt as if they had something special, although she knew the next morning that he was feeling guilty. He'd said he didn't want to lead her on. He'd told her that there was some woman back home he was still in love with. He'd said their night together was a mistake. But he was wrong, and she was determined to convince him of it.

What made it so hard was that Chase was a genuinely nice guy. You didn't let a man like that get away. The other woman had. Fiona wasn't going to make that mistake, even though he'd been trying to push her away since that night. But he had no idea how determined she could be, determined enough for both of them that this wasn't over by a long shot.

It wasn't the first time she'd let herself into his apartment when he was at work. The other time, he'd caught her and she'd had to make up some story about the building manager letting her in so she could look for her lost earring.

She'd snooped around his house the first night they'd met—the same night she'd found his extra apartment key and had taken it to have her own key made in case she ever needed to come back when Chase wasn't home.

The letter hadn't been in his sock drawer that time.

That meant he'd received it since then. Hadn't she known he was hiding something from her? Why else would he put this letter in a drawer instead of leaving it out along with the bills he'd casually dropped on the table by the front door?

Because the letter was important to him, which meant that she had no choice but to read it.

Don't miss
Steel Resolve *by B.J. Daniels,*
available July 2019 wherever
Harlequin® Intrigue books and ebooks are sold.

www.Harlequin.com

Garrett Sterling brought his horse up short as something across the deep ravine caught his eye. A fierce wind swayed the towering pines against the mountainside as he dug out his binoculars. He could smell the rain in the air. Dark clouds had gathered over the top of Whitefish Mountain. If he didn't turn back soon, he would get caught in the summer thunderstorm. Not that he minded it all that much, except the construction crew working at the guest ranch would be anxious for the weekend and their paychecks. Most in these parts didn't buy into auto deposit.

Even as the wind threatened to send his Stetson flying and he felt the first few drops of rain dampen his long-sleeved Western shirt, he couldn't help being curious about what he'd glimpsed. He'd seen something moving through the trees on the other side of the ravine.

He raised the binoculars to his eyes, waiting for them to focus. "What the hell?" When he'd caught movement, he'd been expecting elk or maybe a deer. If he was lucky, a bear. He hadn't seen a grizzly in this area in a long time, but it was always a good idea to know if one was around.

But what had caught his eye was human. He was too startled to breathe for a moment. A large man moved through the pines. He wasn't alone. He had hold of a woman's wrist in what appeared to be a death grip and was dragging her behind him. She seemed to be struggling to stay on her feet. It was what he saw in the man's other hand that had stolen his breath. A gun.

Garrett couldn't believe what he was seeing. Surely, he was wrong. Through the binoculars, he tried to keep track of the two. But he kept losing them as they moved through the thick pines. His pulse pounded as he considered what to do.

His options were limited. He was too far away to intervene and he had a steep ravine between him and the man with the gun. Nor could he call for help—as if help could arrive in time. There was no cell phone coverage this far back in the mountains outside of Whitefish, Montana.

Through the binoculars, he saw the woman burst out of the trees and realized that she'd managed to break away from the man. For a moment, Garrett thought she was going to get away. But the man was larger and faster and was on her quickly, catching her and jerking her around to face him. He hit her with the gun, then put the barrel to her head as he jerked her to him.

"No!" Garrett cried, the sound lost in the wind and crackle of thunder in the distance. After dropping the binoculars onto his saddle, he drew his sidearm from the holster at his hip and fired a shot into the air. It echoed across the wide ravine, startling his horse.

As he struggled to holster the pistol again and grab the binoculars, a shot from across the ravine filled the air, echoing back at him.

Don't miss
Luck of the Draw *by B.J. Daniels, available June 2019*
wherever Harlequin® books and ebooks are sold.

www.Harlequin.com